A STANDALONE NOVELLA

NEW YORK TIMES BESTSELLING AUTHOR
DEBORAH
BLADON

FIRST ORIGINAL EDITION, JANUARY 2017

Copyright © 2017 by Deborah Bladon

ISBN-13: 978-1542327541
ISBN-10: 1542327547
eBook ISBN: 978-1-926440-42-2

Book & cover design by Wolf & Eagle Media

www.deborahbladon.com

Also by Deborah Bladon

Chapter 1

Lark

"How big do you think it is, Lark?"

"I think it's average, but I'm not the best judge when it comes to stuff like this." I smile at my co-worker, Dexie Walsh. "Everyone thinks I'm the expert, but seriously, I have no idea."

"Who thinks you're the expert?" She applies a thin layer of pink stained gloss to her lips. "I know your stats. If we're going by that, I'm more of an expert than you are."

My stats? The only statistic that matters when we're talking about our end of the year bonus is my relationship to the Chief Operating Officer of Matiz Cosmetics. My older brother, Crew, signs those checks and he's been tight-lipped about what's inside the envelopes he's going to hand out at this meeting. All I know for certain is that my check will be the same amount as every other junior executive who works in marketing for the company. No special favors are granted to me. The fact that I didn't get a bonus at all last year is proof of that.

"My brother is responsible for the bonuses." I finger one of the buttons on the front of the navy blue dress I'm wearing. "That fact alone means I'm more of an expert than you'll ever be."

"Who the hell is talking about bonuses?" She leans closer to me, lowering her voice. "I'm talking about Mr. Moore's dick."

I squirm in my seat, resisting the urge to cover both of my ears with my hands. This is not a conversation that's suitable for the boardroom. I'm not going to talk about Ryker Moore's nude photo scandal at this conference table. Ten of our co-workers are here. They're all within earshot and even if Dexie and I whisper they'll know what we're talking about.

It's been the primary discussion topic for the past two days. Everyone in the office, except for most of the men, has been focused on the candid shots of Mr. Moore and his girlfriend that were posted online last Friday night. I thought that people might forget about them over the weekend, but that didn't happen. Bright and early Monday morning I arrived at the office to see several of my co-workers huddled together whispering and staring at the screen of a phone.

Those pictures left nothing to the imagination. The two people in the photos were completely naked and apparently unaware that they were being photographed.

"I'm not talking about this." I elbow Dexie as I shoot her a look. "How would you feel if someone took naked pictures of you and posted them online without your permission?"

"I'd send them a fruit basket and my latest purse as a great big thank you." She laughs. "If it takes flashing a camera to get more eyes on my line of handbags, I'm up for it."

I think she's kidding about going nude for publicity, but I wouldn't put it past her. Dexie works at Matiz for two reasons and two reasons only. She's using the bulk of her pay to fund her burgeoning handmade purse business, and she's soaking up all the marketing knowledge that our boss, Ryker Moore, is always dishing out.

He's a genius when it comes to selling cosmetics. That's impressive on its own, but before he came on board as the head of marketing here, he helped Liore Lingerie reach a billion dollar in sales. My brother thinks Mr. Moore can shoot Matiz's numbers into the stratosphere.

"You'll catch a break one of these days, Dexie," I say as I eye the doorway expecting Crew to walk in at any second. "I've been sharing all of your designs on my social media accounts. I don't have a ton of followers yet, but every little bit helps, right?"

"I can't argue with that." She starts to sketch something with a pencil on the notepad in front of her. "My time will come."

"Speaking of time," I segue awkwardly. "Crew is late. This meeting was supposed to start at ten, wasn't it? It's almost ten-thirty."

She glances up at the circular clock hanging over the doorway. "The email Crew sent out specifically said that we all had to be in the boardroom at ten or risk having to get him coffee for the entire month of January. He never follows through on those threats, does he?"

The only person he'd order to get him coffee would be me, but he knows that I'll flip him the bird in response. Working at Matiz under the watchful eye of one of my three older brothers has been both a blessing and a curse.

I'm grateful knowing that Crew always has my back even if I've told him on more than one occasion that I want to be treated the same as every other employee in the organization. He's done exactly that since I started working here thirteen months ago. We may be siblings, but I'm making a name for myself as one of the most innovative members of the marketing team. Knowing that he's in the same building as me every day offers a sense of comfort that I've never admitted to him I need.

"Did either of you see this one?"

I immediately turn to my left toward the voice of Christine Smith. We were hired within a week of each other. She's holding her smartphone in her hand, the image on the screen an all too familiar one of Mr. Moore on a Caribbean beach last week. Dexie glances at it briefly before she directs her attention back to the sketch she's working on.

"Put that away, Christine." I nudge her with my shoulder. "If Crew catches you looking at that during work hours, he'll reprimand you."

"I wish." She swipes her thumb over the screen of her phone to bring up a meme made from one of the nude photos of Mr. Moore. A cartoon tongue is hiding everything a swimsuit should have been. "I'd seriously burn the building to the ground if it meant your brother would take me over his knee and give my ass a good swat."

"Gross," I say the word with a light chuckle. "Don't talk about Crew that way and stop staring at Mr. Moore's pictures. You know those pictures are an invasion of his privacy, don't you?"

"I know these pictures are what I look at when I'm having some private time with my battery operated boyfriend."

I try to stifle a laugh. "I don't get the fascination but to each her own."

"Who do you think you're fooling?" She turns in her chair as she lowers her tone. "His cock has to be at least nine inches, Lark. I've never been with anyone bigger than a seven. He was a thin seven who had no idea what he was doing. Ryker's working with some serious equipment and I get the impression that he knows how to handle every thick inch of it."

"I don't think about things like that," I half-lie. I'm not about to admit that I stared at the pictures when they first went viral. It's not every day you see your gorgeous boss completely nude.

Christine moves her thumb across the screen of her phone yet again. "Who do you think you're fooling? Every single woman in this room has rubbed one out to those pictures."

I look around the table before my gaze falls back on her phone. The meme that's now on display has a rainbow that ends right between Mr. Moore's legs. Whoever made that one obviously thinks my boss's dick is a treasure.

"I seriously doubt most of the women in this room have seen the pictures, Christine."

"Let's find out." She spins her phone in her hand, so the screen is now facing the center of the conference table. "If you're a man close your eyes. If you're a woman, raise your hand if you saw this picture or any picture of Mr. Moore with no pants on."

More than a few people burst out laughing and two hands dart into the air before they fly back down.

"Stop it, Christine." I reach for her phone, but she's taller than me, which means her arms are longer than mine. My hand flails in the air. "No one needs to see that."

"Calm down, Lark." She waves the phone in front of her. "Everyone wants to see what's at the end of this rainbow."

"No, they don't." I push myself to my feet and yank her phone from her hand. "It's just a penis. It's not a pot of gold."

Raucous laughter fills the room until his words cut through it all. "Ms. Benton? What exactly are you doing?"

I cringe when I hear his voice. I'd know it anywhere. It's masculine, naturally authoritative and it belongs to my boss. I place Christine's phone on the table before I look to the doorway where Mr. Moore is standing with a stack of envelopes in his hands.

"Nothing." I lower myself into my chair. "I wasn't doing anything."

"That's debatable." His lips curve into a slight smirk. "Crew was called to the store in Midtown, so I'll be taking over the meeting today. No one has a problem with that, do they?"

His eyes haven't left mine since I looked at him. Damn Christine and her phone for putting me in that position and damn Ryker Moore and his utterly perfect face and body for making me feel like the room is suddenly one hundred degrees. It doesn't matter that he's dressed in a bespoke black suit. I know what's under it. We all do.

"I'll need a moment after the meeting in my office, Lark." He studies me as he takes a seat at the head of the table. "There's a small matter we need to discuss."

"A small matter?" Christine whispers in my ear. "Nothing about him that matters is small."

I bite my bottom lip to keep from smiling as I nod. "I'll be there, sir."

Chapter 2

Lark

"The bonus was very generous, Mr. Moore," I say an hour later as he closes the door to his office behind me. "I realize you don't have final say in the amount, but I'm glad that it's marginally more than the one that was given out last year."

One of his dark brows peaks at my subtle burn. I respect Ryker Moore for the job he's doing at Matiz, but he hasn't carved out a place for himself next to my brother yet. Crew is Ryker's boss and although I'd never use that to my personal advantage, I know it can't hurt to remind him, particularly in a moment like this.

There's no business-related reason for this meeting. Every promotional campaign that I've been assigned to help manage is either running smoothly or wrapped and ready to go. The only open file is a mascara campaign for next fall which is still in the very early planning stages.

"Sit, Lark." He barks the order out as he points to a chair in front of his desk.

I lower myself into the leather chair as I watch his face for any sign of what he's about to say. He's stoic. His blue eyes give nothing away. His strong jaw is set firm. The only thing out of place is a lock of black hair that has fallen onto his forehead.

"Why am I here?" I ask with a slight tilt of my head. "I dropped off the files for the spring launch of the new lipstick with your assistant yesterday."

"I got those." He taps his long fingers on the flash drive I stored everything on. "You never cease to impress me, Lark. You have a pulse on the market."

I should. I wear only Matiz products. I did that long before I landed a job here after graduating from college. I know how I feel when I walk out of my apartment with Matiz make-up on. I want every woman to feel that same sense of confidence I do when I know I look my best.

I may have gray eyes and blonde hair, but that's never equated to natural beauty to me. I went through the same awkward acne and breakout stage almost every young woman has. I struggled with liking what I saw in the mirror. The cosmetics Crew gave me for my birthday the past few years have helped but it was learning to love myself that made the difference. I'm still working on that. I'm not perfect, but I'm enough for me.

"Thank you for recognizing that," I say with a smile. "I think the new campaigns are going to blow the competition out of the water."

"I agree." He leans forward, his elbows resting on the desk. "You've done well. You're an important part of the team."

I rest my back against the chair, relief flowing through me. I highly doubt that I was summoned here because of my recent work. I know it's stellar. I don't need Ryker or my brother to tell me that, but it's still good to hear. "Did you ask me here to talk about the holiday campaign for next year?"

It's a longshot but I want in on that campaign. I have ideas that I believe will catapult sales of Matiz products. I was passed over this year because I was still considered a rookie. I've proven my worth over the last quarter.

He pauses. "I'll be making a decision on the team for next year's holiday campaign in the new year. I haven't given it any thought yet."

I curse inwardly. The legitimate business related reasons for this meeting are quickly narrowing to zero. Ever since he walked into the conference room and heard me talking about his penis, I've been dreading any conversation between us that would involve that. I've tried to convince myself that he won't bring it up. He has to be embarrassed that the pictures were released. There's no way in hell he'd want to talk about them.

"Please keep me in mind," I reply, hoping to drag out our stunted discussion about a campaign that is months away from the planning stages. "If we're done here, I'd like to get back to my desk."

"We're not done."

I don't look at him because frankly I can't right now. Obviously, eye contact is inevitable when you work in close collaboration with someone, but I've gotten good at avoiding it as much as possible since that night almost a year ago.

I couldn't avoid looking at him in the conference room earlier when he walked in right when I was talking about his cock. I don't have to stare at him now even though the temptation to do just that is almost irresistible.

"It was evident in the boardroom earlier that you were discussing the pictures of Gem and me that were posted online last week."

Gem. The name doesn't suit the woman who bears it. Ryker's girlfriend is a social media darling. Her ass is technically the star of her Instagram account. She's used her body to gain close to twenty million followers and several lucrative sponsorship deals with big name companies, including Matiz. She wears our products exclusively in the images that do show her face. Those postings aren't as frequent as the ones of her in a bikini or work-out gear but every time she shares the name of one of our lipsticks or eye shadows, the product sells out in record time.

"Everyone is discussing those pictures," I say evenly. "I was actually trying to get Christine to stop talking about them when you walked in."

"That's where the pot of gold comment came from?"

I should thank him for not bringing up the fact that I said the word *penis* in a corporate setting but technically it's his fault that I did. If he had kept his swimsuit on, no one would have seen his cock, including me.

"Yes," I answer quickly. "I was trying to explain to her that they're just pictures."

"They're just pictures?" he asks darkly, his face stoic. "If they were pictures of you, would you consider them just pictures?"

"I can't answer that question because I'd never put myself in such a compromising position."

If he's going to push, I'm going to shove. I have no problem walking around naked at home. I keep my blinds closed and the camera on my laptop covered with a piece of electrical tape. I'm safe there. The last thing I would ever do is strip in broad daylight.

"You'd never put yourself in a compromising position?" His gaze narrows. "Are you sure about that, Lark?"

Chapter 3

Lark

My heart thumps a beat so loud I'd bet half of Manhattan can hear it. I know that he doesn't remember what happened at the Christmas party last year, so I need to calm the hell down. He's not talking about the kiss we shared under what I think was mistletoe, although it had the distinct odor of cilantro. He's never brought up that night because he was too drunk to remember it.

"I'm sure," I mutter as I stand. I think I'm sure. I *hope* I'm sure.

He pauses to consider what I just said as if he doesn't believe my words. "I'd like you to refrain from discussing the pictures while you're in the office."

"I have no intention of ever discussing those pictures again," I blurt out so quickly that my words tumble into each other. "I have no reason to talk about your pictures, so I won't. I won't do it here at the office or when I'm at home or anywhere else."

Shut the hell up, Lark. Just shut up already.

"My concern is the office." He scoops his phone into his palm. "What you discuss after hours is your business. I can't police that."

"I won't be talking about your… I mean, I have no reason to talk about your…" I fumble for the right words, preferably any that don't include a reference to his dick. "I won't be talking about your pictures again."

"Fine." He looks at the screen of his phone. "You're free to go. I assume I'll see you at the marketing party tomorrow night?"

I'll be there with bells on. I'll literally have bells on since the dress I bought for the occasion has two bells attached to the sash. "I'll be there."

Just as I turn toward the door of his office, my phone chime cuts through the air. I ignore it even though it's in my hand.

"You have a new message," he says from behind me. "It might be important."

Or it might be another reminder that I'm a month overdue for my dentist checkup. "It's nothing."

"It's something, Lark."

I pivot on my heel so I'm facing him directly again. "I think I would know if it was important. I assure you that it's nothing."

"Humor me and have a look." He points to my phone. "I guarantee this is something you'll want to see."

"Fine," I groan as I open the text message app on my phone to find his name at the top of the list. He sent me a photo less than thirty seconds ago. "What's this?"

"It's the consequence of you putting yourself in a compromising position."

I have no idea what the hell that's supposed to mean so I do the only thing I can. I open the message and scroll down until the attached photo pops into view.

"How?" I whisper under my breath as I stare at a picture of the small heart shaped tattoo that's on the inside of my left thigh. "You can't have a picture of this. Where did you get this?"

He sighs as his fingers glide over his phone's screen.

"Tell me where you got this." I wave my phone in his direction as my face heats. "Are there cameras installed in the women's washroom? If there are, that's illegal. I'm calling the police."

My phone chimes again just as he speaks. "This next picture might jar your memory. Take a look."

Next picture? How many goddamn pictures of my bare thigh does this man have?

My hands shake as I open the message he apparently just sent. There's a photo attached to this one as well. I scroll down, my breath catching as the image comes into view.

My tattoo is the focus of this one too, but there's more. The pink lace panties I'm wearing are visible. The fact that they're slightly askew means a sliver of my pussy is on display. I was obviously on my back in this picture since my face is partially visible in the distance.

Holy shit. No. No. No.

I cradle the phone to my chest, blocking the screen from his view even though he's obviously already seen both pictures. "How did you get these? Who gave them to you?"

He stands, his fingers buttoning his suit jacket. "At the holiday party a year ago you announced to the room that you were uploading all the pictures you'd taken of the festivities to a gallery on the company's server."

I remember that. I'd just started working at Matiz a month before the party. I wanted to do something nice for my co-workers so I used my phone to snap dozens of pictures during the party of everyone enjoying the food and appetizers.

"Apparently I was the only one listening to you," he goes on. "I checked out the gallery later that night, and to my surprise, you'd uploaded those two very personal pictures along with the images you took of your intoxicated co-workers."

I swallow past the large lump in my throat. "I uploaded those two pictures to the company server?"

He rounds his desk and approaches me. "You uploaded them, and I deleted them. I doubt anyone had a look at them before I removed them."

I should thank him, right? I should thank him for keeping my pussy private.

"I had no idea I did that," I manage to say.

"I assumed it was a mistake, Lark. You did have more than your fair share of red wine that night." He strokes his chin, his eyes studying my face. "I highly doubted that you'd deliberately compromise yourself that way."

Is this a lesson? Is he throwing my words back in my face? What a jerk. What a distractingly good-looking jerk.

"I appreciate you looking out for me." I twist my mouth into what I hope resembles a half-assed genuine grin. "Thank you for deleting them from the server."

His lips purse and I wonder for a brief second if he's going to kiss me again. It only happened once under that cilantro scented mistletoe. I've wanted it to happen again ever since but he hooked up with Gem, the ultimate social media ass. Or she has the ultimate ass according to social media. Either way, he was kissing her and not me by the end of January. They've been on and off over the course of the last year but it didn't make any difference in my life. Everything between us since our one and only kiss has been all business.

His phone rings. He answers it quickly. I don't hear the words he's saying. I'm too busy staring at my phone.

I took these two pictures of my tattoo for a guy I broke up with before I started working here. I scrubbed my phone of every reminder of him when he texted me last Valentine's Day out of the blue wanting to hook up. I don't have those pictures anymore yet Mr. Moore still does.

I tap him on the shoulder as he speaks to someone about the upcoming trends in eyebrow pencils. "Mr. Moore, I have to ask you something."

He shoots me a look accompanied by a thrust of his index finger in the air.

Is that supposed to be a warning for me to be quiet?

I shake my head. "This is urgent."

He presses his phone to the front of his suit jacket to block out our conversation from the person he's talking to. "I'm in the middle of an important call, Lark. Whatever it is, will need to wait. You're excused."

I'm excused? Does he think this is fifth grade? I move past him and sit back down in the chair I was in earlier. "I'll wait until you're done."

"You'll leave now."

"I can't," I say with a tremor in my voice. "I need you to explain something to me."

"This call is important, Lark." He moves to my side. "It requires my attention. Please leave."

I look up at his face. He's serious, deadly serious. I don't want any part of this conversation to get back to Crew, so I haul my ass back out of the chair and face him. "I'll go, but I need to speak with you as soon as possible."

"Fine." He waves his hand in the direction of his door. "See yourself out."

I curse under my breath as I open the door, walk through and slam it shut behind me.

Chapter 4

Ryker

Crew Benton's younger sister is everything I'm not supposed to want. She works for me. She's related to my boss. She's got the sweetest smile I've ever seen, and she smells like she took a bath in a mountain spring. She's innocence personified. She's not my usual type at all unless you consider that tattoo on her thigh.

That damn small heart tattoo that has haunted me since I first saw those two pictures a year ago.

I knew immediately it was her when I scanned that ridiculous gallery of pictures she'd uploaded the night of the Christmas party. I imagine her intention was to gain someone's favor by capturing the evening's events. The only reason I scrolled through the images on the laptop in my office was to delete any of me.

I had a few too many beers as I shot the shit with the employees who run their asses off every single day for me. I had somewhere else to be, but when I saw Lark standing in the corner alone, I couldn't remember anything.

I got a small taste of what I wanted for Christmas when I kissed her under that cilantro some idiot bought as a pass-off for mistletoe. It was hung near the elevators, and when I walked out of the crowded conference room to see Lark standing beneath it, I caved.

I craved a taste of those perfectly shaped, full, pink lips. I got it when she turned, tilted her neck back and offered her mouth to me after I tapped her on the shoulder and pointed at the cilantro. We didn't exchange a single word, just a kiss that I've never forgotten. She broke the kiss when the elevator doors flew open, and two of her co-workers stepped off. She stepped on and was gone in a flash.

"Ryker? What the fuck is going on between you and Lark?"

Daydreams about a woman you want to screw should never be interrupted by her brother. Why the fuck did I agree when Human Resources told me that Lark was a great fit for the marketing division? I thought I'd be able to look past how attractive she is. I was confident that I'd be able to ignore the way she looks at me. It's been a struggle every single day since I met her.

"Hey, Crew," I shoot those two words off my tongue with as much cheeriness as I can muster. "What's up?"

He stands in the doorway of my office. He bears no resemblance at all to Lark. She's a blonde. His hair is as black as mine. Her eyes are a shade of soft shade of gray. His are green. There's no way to tell they're related based on appearance. The only similarity between the two of them is their effort to distance themselves from the Benton name. Their parents own half the real estate in Manhattan, yet neither of them works for them. I've overheard Crew grumbling to Nolan Black, the co-owner of Matiz, about how controlling his father is. The elder Benton has to be a fucking tyrant if two of his four children want nothing to do with him professionally.

"Word around the office is that you ordered Lark in here after the meeting this morning." He doesn't hesitate as he steps toward me. "Why?"

I scramble for something to say that isn't related to my dick pictures or that photo that shows the barest slice of her smooth pussy.

"We were discussing the holiday party for our division."

Not a complete lie. We talked about last year's party.

"You're fucking fired if you told her about the surprise, Ryker." His eyes narrow on me. "Tell me you didn't spill the beans."

"What beans?" I shoot back when I realize the grin on his face means he's kidding about firing me. "I don't know what you're talking about."

"You play dumb well, Moore." He taps my chest with his finger. "You did this same song and dance with her, right? Tell me that she still thinks there's an office Christmas party tomorrow night."

I still think there's an office Christmas party tomorrow night. I had plans to be there. I've vowed to steer clear of any beverages that are stronger than water and anything that resembles mistletoe. I may be single since I dumped Gem, but Lark Benton is still on my I-wish-I-could-fuck-but-I-can't list.

"She thinks there's an office party tomorrow," I say smoothly. "She has no idea about the surprise."

"Good," he replies over his shoulder as he turns to leave. "My baby sister deserves the surprise birthday party of her dreams. I don't want a soul to fuck it up."

***

"Christmas Day?" I repeat back to my assistant. "Lark Benton was born on Christmas Day?"

"She's a Christmas angel." He gives me a sly smirk. "She's beautiful. I wouldn't say she's as beautiful as Crew, but he's more my type."

I don't need him to elaborate on that. I've caught him checking me out on more than one occasion. John does his job like a champ. He proved that just now when he pulled up Lark's personnel file for me just as Crew was stepping onto the elevator to go back up to his office. This is one time I'm grateful that he overheard my conversation with Crew.

"Did you know about this surprise birthday party, John?"

"I'm out of the loop." He circles his fingers in the air. "Everyone who is anyone here at Matiz knows I swore off mixing business with pleasure years ago. I don't socialize with the folks here. No one in this office can party as hard as I can, present company excluded, of course."

I nod. "You need to find out where this birthday party is."

"You're not going, Ryker."

What the fuck is that? I go where I want when I want. I'm going to that damn birthday party because I'm her boss and I should be there. It's the right thing to do. It has nothing to do with wanting to see her outside the office. There's no reason I can't look at her. I'm beginning to wonder if my reasons for not touching her are worth it.

"I'm going," I insist as I lean both hands on his desk. "You're going to poke around until you find out where that party is and then you'll chat up her friends in marketing to find out what flowers are her favorite so I can arrive at this party with those in my hand."

"You'll never pass for Prince Charming." He types something on his laptop keyboard. "Are you taking Gem with you?"

"I dumped her."

"Again?" He stops typing long enough to clap his hands together before his fingers move swiftly over the keys again. "Can I wager a bet on how long it will be before you're back together?"

"We're done for good this time." I pinch the bridge of my nose. "I need you to focus on Lark's party. You'll get me that information now, John. I need it within the hour."

"Will do, boss." He reaches down to open one of the drawers of his desk. He pulls out a gift bag that's decorated with a festive design and tied shut with red ribbon. "I got you this as an early Christmas gift."

36

"Your gift from me will be delivered to your apartment on Christmas morning," I tell him, not giving anything away with my expression. The gift is his mom. I'm flying her to New York from Tallahassee. She'll deliver a message to him from me. He has two weeks to spend with her before she flies back home. I'm giving him an extra week of paid vacation that he's not expecting.

"What's this?" I reach for the bag, contemplating its weight in my hand. "It's not another book about how to forge meaningful human connections, is it?"

"That was obviously a waste of money." He scoffs. "It's a bottle of Matiz's best suntan lotion. Slap some of that on your ass the next time you let everything hang loose on the beach, boss."

"I should fire you on the spot." I chuckle.

"You can't," he volleys back as I head into my office. "No one else would put up with all your bullshit, Ryker."

Chapter 5

Lark

"Everyone at work was acting off today." I toss my purse on the marbled gray granite countertop. "It's been a shitty two days, Isla."

My best friend, Isla Foster, scoops my purse into her hands. "Where is this from? I've never seen this before."

"Way to console me after the two bad days I've had." I wiggle two of my fingers in the air. "Where's my *'everything is going to be fine, Lark,'* speech and hug."

"That's coming." She twirls the red tote in her hands. "This isn't a designer bag. Tell me where you got it. I want one."

"Dexie made it." I tug it from her hands and dump the contents on her kitchen counter. "You can have it, Isla. Dex gave me a new one as an early birthday present the other day. It's a cute purple satchel."

"Dexie? That girl you work with made this bag?"

"Yup." I nod my head as I push my wallet into my coat pocket. "Her designs are beautiful. She sells them online. I can send you the link to her website."

"Send it." She shoulders the bag. "Are you ready for the Matiz holiday party tonight?"

"No," I answer truthfully. "I'm not sure I'm going."

"You're going."

"It's not a mandatory work thing. It's just a small get-together for people who work in marketing." I eye an apple in a fruit bowl. "Maybe I'll just eat that apple for dinner and go home and watch Christmas movies while I stuff my face with popcorn."

She picks up the apple and tosses it to me. "Eat it and then go home and get dressed. You'll regret not going to the party, Lark."

"Why would I regret it?"

She smooths her ponytail with her hand, pushing a few wayward strands of her long blonde hair back into place. "If you don't go to that party, the people you work with will assume that you think you're above them because of who your brother is. Don't set yourself apart from them, Lark. Prove that you're just like all of them."

I try to push a lipstick into my pocket, but there's no room. "I'm not just like all of them. I know they say things about me behind my back. I thought it would be easy working at Matiz, but it's not, Isla. I'm not even sure that anyone there genuinely likes me for me."

"You're just feeling sorry for yourself. Your twenties are slipping away from you. You'll be twenty-four in a few days." She rests her hands on my shoulders. "I'll feel the same way on my twenty-fourth birthday in a few months. I'll have my own pity party as I kiss my youth goodbye."

I burst out laughing. "You're hilarious. You have a perfect life. You're killing it at Juilliard. You're married to Gabriel Foster and you have a beautiful daughter. You're the last person who will ever throw themselves a pity party."

"I do have the perfect life." She stares at her wedding rings. "Gabriel is taking me to Italy in the spring. It's my Christmas gift. He told me last night. We'll take Ella with us. He called in some favors so I can play my violin with one of my idols in Tuscany. It's a dream come true."

Since I met Isla eight months ago while we were both standing in line at a coffee shop, I've never envied her. I've always been happy for her and the life she's built for herself. I want a life that fulfills me too, but a husband and a baby girl aren't in the cards for me yet. I'll settle for a night at home alone hidden under the covers of my bed. I'm still embarrassed about those two images of my tattoo Mr. Moore sent me yesterday.

"Promise me you'll take lots of pictures." I cup her chin in my hand. "Promise me you'll be safe there."

"I'll guard her with my life." Gabriel strolls into the kitchen with his daughter on his hip. "I won't let Isla or Ella out of my sight. Italy is just the beginning of our adventures."

I reach forward to plant a kiss on Ella's cheek. "I have a gift for Ella for Christmas. Can I drop it off tomorrow?"

"No." Isla shakes her head. "I thought you were spending part of Christmas Day with us. It's your birthday, Lark. I'm going to bake a cake."

"We're going to order a cake from Dobb's bakery for you," Gabriel interjects. "Isla will pick up a pint of mint, chocolate chip ice cream from Cremza too."

The fact that he remembers my favorite ice cream shop and flavor touches me. I have three brothers of my own, but Gabriel has proven in both words and actions, that he has the emotional capacity to love anyone his wife does. He may be one of the shrewdest businessmen in all of Manhattan, but his heart is as soft as Isla's is.

"Stop by after dinner at your parent's house on Christmas Day, Lark." Isla tugs at my hand. "Come over and have dessert with us."

"Deal." I scoop my phone, my lipstick and my compact mirror into my hands. "I have to go get ready for the party I don't want to go to."

"You know about the party?" Gabriel arches a dark brow. "I thought it was…"

"He thought it was tomorrow night," Isla interrupts. "He can't keep his days straight anymore. That's what old age does to a hot man."

43

He huffs out a laugh. "You'll pay for that later, Isla."

"Promise?" She turns to him. "Promise I'll pay for it."

"That's my cue to leave." I run my hand over Ella's brow. "I'll see you in a few days, little lovely."

***

"You weren't at the party last year." I adjust the collar of Crew's dress shirt. "Why are you making an appearance this year?"

He studies my face. "When did you grow up?"

"It's been a long time coming." I step back to survey the shirt. It's flawless. "You didn't answer my question. You weren't at the marketing department's holiday party last year. Why are you going with me this year?"

"Things were fucked up last year. Ryker was only on the job for a few months back then. I'd fired Miller, the idiot who used to head marketing, right before Thanksgiving. Every person who works in that department wanted my head on a platter because they loved Miller and I passed them over for the promotion and gave it to Ryker." He rubs his forehead. "It was a shit show, Lark. I stayed away for my own personal safety."

"I only want to stay for an hour," I announce, ignoring his long winded accounting of why he stood me up last year. He was with a woman. I don't need to be a genius to figure that out. My brother doesn't hide the fact that he has a penchant for beautiful brunettes. Everyone who works at Matiz knows it. "After that, I'm coming back here to watch Christmas movies and drink egg nog."

"You're going to be twenty-four in a few days, Lark, not eighty-four. You've been single since your ex moved to L.A. Why don't you hit a club after the party? You're looking stellar tonight in your Mrs. Claus getup."

I look down at the plaid dress I'm wearing. It's red and black with a white belt complete with those two small bells attached to the buckle. "What's wrong with my dress?"

"Nothing if you're trying to attract an old white haired stalker type with a beard who creeps around the world in the darkness of night dressed in a red suit."

"I'm trying to be festive. I found this at a vintage shop in the West Village."

He eyes me again. "You're beautiful. I think you're too beautiful. It scares the hell out of me that you look the way you do. Even in this tablecloth dress you look like a million bucks."

"My dress looks like a tablecloth?"

He nods. "Granny Benton had a tablecloth that matched this. I think it's the same material."

"Shit." I cover my eyes with my hands. "That's why I fell in love with it. It reminded me of Granny Benton."

"Go change." He points toward my bedroom. "Choose something less Granny and more millennial."

"I don't have time." I glance at the watch on his wrist. "It's almost seven, isn't it? The party starts at seven."

"Who the hell cares when it starts?" He scoffs with a grin. "I'm the fucking boss, sis. Take all the time you need. The party won't start until we walk through the door."

Chapter 6

Lark

"Do you know what Mr. Moore's been working on the last couple of days?" I ask as I stare out the window of the car that was waiting outside my apartment building for us. My brother is an Uber or taxi type of guy, but tonight he opted for a chauffeur driven sedan. He must have a date after the Christmas party. I've learned the hard way never to ask questions about his personal life.

"Mr. Moore?" he mimics my voice as he repeats Ryker's name. "What the fuck is that? Does he make you call him that?"

"I call him that because that's his name."

"His name is Ryker. You should call him that." He taps my knee. "Don't bow down to him, Lark. He's your superior, but you're gaining on him. Some of your ideas crush his."

I can't tell if he's being genuine or being an older brother. I choose the former because the ego boost never hurts. I look at the driver before I bring my attention to Crew. "I've needed to speak to him since yesterday, but he's been out of his office. His assistant said he was busy with a special project."

"Special project?" He looks at me with skepticism in his eyes.

"It's probably Gem." My voice is a murmur.

"Gem?" he repeats back almost instantly. "That's over, Lark. She dumped him a couple of days ago."

"She did?" I try not to sound as excited as I feel. I don't know why my heart jumps at the news but it does.

Ryker has shown limited interest in me since the kiss we shared a year ago. Sometimes I feel like he's looking at me like I'm a woman and he's a man instead of the way a boss looks at his employee, but he's hard to read. Besides, Gem is always floating in and out of his life. I got so tired of seeing pictures of them together online, that I stopped searching for either of their names.

"She's throwing him under the bus." He pushes his phone into my lap.

I glance down. It's a profile on a social media site. I know instantly, based on the seductive photo of a brunette in a bikini that it belongs to Gem. I scroll down and see a few postings that mention Ryker. I only read two before I give the phone back to Crew. "Some things need to be private."

"You're telling me. Like those pictures of the two of them on the beach." He leans forward to gaze through the windshield. "I'm waiting for her to talk shit about Matiz. If that happens, one of our company lawyers is ready to pounce."

Everything is business to Crew. He protects the Matiz name even though the bulk of the company is owned by his closest friend, Nolan Black. Crew would fight off a lion with his bare hands if it meant Matiz kept its good name. He's loyal to those he loves. He's going to be an amazing husband to a lucky woman one day.

"Why didn't we turn on Fifth Avenue?" I glance back out the window. "We're headed away from Matiz. We can't go to the party if we're going in the wrong direction."

The driver chuckles but he doesn't offer any explanation.

"I moved the party to Nova," Crew says nonchalantly. "The food is better."

"Nova?" I push my back into the car's seat. "The restaurant owned by Tyler Monroe? We're having the marketing party at Nova?"

"We are." His eyes gleam. "I think it's a much better choice than potato chips and cheap beer and wine in the boardroom."

"It's also way more expensive," I counter. "You're telling me you're paying for a party at Nova? Crew Benton is hosting a party for his employees at Nova? This isn't real."

"It's real, Lark." He gestures out the window as the car slows as it nears the curb. "We're going to spend the evening enjoying food prepared personally by Tyler Monroe."

Holy shit. I love Tyler Monroe. I also love his fiancée, Cadence. I've seen them both on television too many times to count.

They're two of the most talented chefs in the country. I've never been to Nova. I've wanted to go for months but dining alone at an upscale restaurant isn't my thing. I always imagined I'd be on the arm of a handsome man when I had dinner there. I never thought that man would be my brother.

***

"I told you this was a stupid fucked up idea, Crew. She's going to pass out. She's going to fucking pass out because you scared the hell out of her."

I swat my brother Kade across the chest as he leans over me. He's older than me but younger than Crew. He speaks before he thinks but tonight he's going to tone it down. Acting like an asshole at my party isn't allowed.

"I'm just surprised," I say as I look up at Crew and Kade. "I didn't know this was my birthday party."

I couldn't have known. When I walked through the door of Nova, I did it with the anticipation of seeing everyone I work with. I never expected to hear people screaming the word '*surprise,*' and I couldn't have known that my parents, my brother, Isla and Gabriel would be standing right in front of me. There are more people here, but those were the faces I recognized before my knees gave out and I fell back into Crew's arms.

"I told Crew this was a bad idea, Lark." Kade brushes his lips over my forehead. "I told him we should keep things as is and toast to your birthday during Christmas dinner. It's what you expect. I only want what's best for you."

They both want what's best for me. All of my brothers do. That's why my mother shoved a birthday card into my hand the moment I sat down. I know it's from Curtis, my eldest brother. He's in Philadelphia for a few days with his family celebrating the holidays early with his in-laws. He'll arrive in New York by train on Christmas Eve with his wife and two boys in tow. The next day my family will open gifts and sing carols and then at the end of the night, my dad will pop open a bottle of champagne and my family will toast to my birthday. It's been that way for as long as I can remember. The champagne used to be sparkling apple juice but the sentiment was always the same. I never got an extra gift. The birthday cakes were eventually replaced with apple and pumpkin pies with a single white candle in the center of each that I blew out after everyone sang *Happy Birthday* to me.

"I brought a glass of water." A deep voice behind me startles me. "It's for the birthday girl."

I turn and look into the very recognizable face of Chef Tyler Monroe. "You're him."

"I'm Tyler," he says as he crouches next to me. "Drink this. You look white as a ghost."

I take the glass from him and down the water in one gulp. "Is your fiancée here? I love her."

"I love her too." He taps the center of his chest with his fingers. "Crew made a special request for her to be here, so she is. Cadence is in the back cooking up a storm for our special guest."

"For me?" I look past his face to Crew's. "This is all for me?"

"All for you, Lark." Crew smiles down at me. "This is your night."

Chapter 7

Ryker

I'm stopped at the door of Nova by a brawny looking bouncer type. I know this place is sitting at the top of everyone's best restaurant in New York list, but the guy dressed in all black with the pissed off look on his face is overkill.

"The restaurant is closed to the public tonight," he says in a thick Russian accent. "You'll come back another night."

"I'll stay tonight," I shoot back with a fake grin. "I'm here for the Benton birthday party."

He gives me the once over. I'm dressed in a black suit, white shirt, and a blue tie. I look the part of the distinguished party guest, even though I was never formally invited. "I'll check the list. What's your name?"

Fuck. Seriously? A guest list?

I look past him into the restaurant to where Crew is standing next to a petite blonde woman. I recognize her immediately. She's Isla Foster. I used to work for her husband, Gabriel, at Liore Lingerie. I'd see her around the office every once in a while, and when I started working for Matiz, she popped up there. We laughed about it at the time before she explained that Lark is her best friend.

"Your name?"

I look back at the guy with the accent. He's asked me twice. I need to give him an answer.

I go for broke because this bouquet of peonies in my hand isn't going to look as great tomorrow morning as it does right now. I want to hand them to Lark tonight. "I'm Ryker Moore. Lark works for me."

He nods. "You're not on the list."

"You didn't check a list."

"I have the list in here." He taps his massive forehead. It's more like a five or six head but I'm not about to point that out.

"Check it again," I say louder hoping to draw Isla's attention.

He rolls his eyes. "I checked. You're not on the list."

"I need to give these flowers to Lark for her birthday."

He reaches for them but I back away quickly. There's no way I'm placing these in his paw. He'll crush them without even trying.

"Give them to me." He lunges toward me. "I'll give them to her."

"No fucking way." I shake my head. "I'm handing these to Lark myself. Step aside and let me in."

"Watch the mouth." He places his index finger over his lips. "This is probably why you're not on the list."

"He's on the list." A soft female voice says from behind me. "You can let him in."

I straighten the knot on my tie before I pivot to face her. I hold the flowers out in front of me. "These are for you, Lark. Happy Birthday."

***

I curse everything in the world when I look down at her hand. It's holding tight to the arm of the man next to her. It's not just an average guy. This guy looks like he belongs on the cover of a magazine. Fuck this night and this surprise birthday party.

"These flowers are beautiful." Her cheeks blush pink. "You bought these for me, Mr. Moore?"

"For your birthday." I try not to stare at the man next to her. I should introduce myself but what's the fucking point? He's obviously her boyfriend. I'm her boss. I'm just her goddamn boss. I can't forget that.

"You knew about this party?" Her gaze drifts over my face. "You came to my birthday party to give me these?"

"Yes," I answer dryly. "I wanted you to know how much I appreciate all the valuable work you do at Matiz."

Her face is awash in something, maybe disappointment or confusion. It's possible that she's frustrated that I crashed her party. I wasn't invited. I don't know why the fuck I thought this was a good idea.

She clears her throat. "Thank you for the flowers. I hope you'll at least stay for dinner. Tyler Monroe and his wife are cooking for us."

I have no fucking idea who that is, but I'm game. She wants me to stay, so I will. "I'll stay."

"Good." Her expression brightens. "We were just out getting some air. We're heading back in there now."

I step aside to let her and her date take the lead. Lark walks into the restaurant just as he stops and extends his hand to me. "So you're the infamous Ryker Moore. I've heard a lot about you."

I give his hand a firm shake. "Don't repeat any of it."

He laughs and drops my hand. "I'm Kade Benton. It's great to meet you, man."

It's fucking amazing to meet him too. He's her brother, not her boyfriend. I feel a sense of relief I know I shouldn't, but I can't deny that there's something about Lark that draws me to her like a moth to a flame.

Chapter 8

Lark

I place the fork on the small plate that had a good size piece of white chocolate birthday cake on it not more than three minutes ago. I practically inhaled it after Isla handed it to me. It's not the best cake I've ever had. That recipe belongs to my mom. She used to bake me a chocolate cake every year for my birthday before the masses started demanding pie as a dessert replacement on Christmas Day.

"You like cake." Mr. Moore swipes his finger over the corner of my mouth before he slides it between his lips. "I can see why. This is delicious."

I freeze in place. That felt intimate. It felt incredibly intimate even if wasn't his intention. The entire night I've felt that sensation over and over again.

He sat next to me during dinner, his knee brushing against mine whenever he moved slightly. He picked up my wine glass by mistake and took a sip before handing it back to me and watching intently as I drank from it.

It was white wine. He chuckled when I ordered a glass of red. I laughed too and immediately changed my mind and ordered white. He did the same.

"I like cake," I say to break what I think is sexual tension. He may think it's just me being my typical awkward self, but it feels like more to me. "Ice cream is my favorite, though."

Way to sound your age, Lark.

"I have a soft spot for ice cream myself." He taps his fingers on his dress shirt over his stomach. It has to be rock hard. I saw the outline of his abs in the pictures of him on the beach. I also saw that unmistakable V that only really hot guys have. Well, hot guys who work out like mad. I saw his cock too, but I've been trying to think of that less and the rest of him more. His body is ideal. It's what any woman could ever want and now it's available and so close to me.

"You don't eat ice cream." I reach out to touch the same spot he just did, but I stop myself. "You can't eat ice cream and look like that."

"When your grandparents own the best ice cream shop in the city, you eat ice cream." He scoops up a tiny bit of buttercream icing onto a spoon and brings it to his lips. He licks it slowly.

My mind jumbles. Do women put icing on their nipples? If we were in bed together and I put icing on my nipples, would he lick it off like that? If I put it on my clit, would he suck it off slowly?

I take another sip of white wine hoping it will shut my imagination down.

"The best ice cream shop in Manhattan is Cremza," I say with conviction. "I've been going there once a week for years. I've tried others but I always go back to Cremza."

"Good to know." He grins and I'm sure an angel somewhere weeps because it's so strikingly beautiful.

Dammit, Lark. Get a fucking grip on yourself. It's just a smile.

I push the half-full glass of wine away from me. I know my limit and I've obviously cruised past it, way past it. "I have to work tomorrow. I should probably get home."

He chuckles, the sound deep and raspy. "You can come in late tomorrow, Lark. I'll overlook it."

"You're a prince, Mr. Moore." I rest my hand on his forearm. "You're not as bad as I thought you were."

"I can be bad."

My head snaps up, my eyes widening in surprise. I look directly at him. This is the first moment I've had alone with him all night. It's the ideal time for me to ask him why he still has those pictures of my tattoo on his phone. I need to ask him that. I should ask him that but I don't. "Did you just say you can be bad?"

"I can be bad," he repeats gruffly. "I can be firm, or demanding. I can be many things."

I squirm slightly in my seat, my thighs rubbing together beneath the thin fabric of my black dress. I don't want to jump to the wrong conclusion. He might be talking about work. There's a chance he's not. There's a huge chance that he's talking about sex; bad, firm, and demanding sex.

Not bad exactly. The man can't be bad in bed. I bet he could get me off just by looking at me long enough. Is that an actual thing? Is it even physically possible? I stare at him to test my theory.

"I know I haven't been the best boss to you or anyone in the marketing department at Matiz." My quest for an orgasm is broken just like that. "I'm too demanding at times. There have been a number of situations that I haven't handled in the best way. My resolution for next year is to improve on that."

My resolution for next year is to find another man to crush on. Ryker Moore is all business when it comes to me. I'm so inconsequential to him outside the office that he can't even remember kissing me. He was looking in Crew's direction so often tonight that I should have clued into what was going on by the time the main course was served. He showed up to my surprise party to impress my brother. Simple.

"We can all make improvements, Mr. Moore. I think resolutions are a great way to guide ourselves down a better path."

"Listen to you sounding all grown up and shit." Crew grabs my shoulders from behind. "Are you ready to go, Lark? The car will be here in ten. Kade and I will load up your gifts in the trunk and I'll take you home."

"I'm as ready as I'll ever be." I move to stand, but Ryker is on his feet first, pulling my chair back for me. He had been just as attentive when I took a seat at the table before dinner. "Thank you again for the flowers, Mr. Moore."

"Tell her to drop that, Moore." Crew scoops up a birthday card that's next to my wine glass. "She should be calling you Ryker."

"I agree." He brushes his hand over my forearm. "I've asked Lark several times to call me Ryker."

He has, but I've seen the scowl on his face whenever any of my colleagues refer to him by his first name. I won't set myself apart just because my older brother owns part of the company.

"I'll call him whatever I want." I turn to look at Crew. "It's not a big deal, Crew. Please don't worry about it."

"She's almost as good as you are, Ryker." Crew smirks. "You should watch your back. Lark's gunning for your job."

Great. What a fantastic way to end my birthday. The man I've thought about having sex with for the past year thinks I'm trying to take his job away from him. That seals the deal that Ryker will never want me the way I want him.

Happy Fucking Birthday, Lark.

Chapter 9

Ryker

I was so close to just putting it all out there. I was one sentence away from telling Lark that I wasn't talking about work when I blurted out to her that I can be bad. I can be bad, or dirty, or sensitive and tender when it comes to fucking. I can be anything the woman I'm with needs me to be. With Lark, I know I can be more.

Crew walked up behind her, though. Right when I was about to invite her out for a drink to cap off the night, he stepped into my view. I spit out that bullshit about trying to be a good boss to cover my tracks. I put a spin on my words so he'd avoid catching on that I want nothing more than to take his sister to bed and never let her leave.

This is so many ways of fucked up I can't count them all.

I didn't pursue her after we kissed last winter because I didn't want to risk the job. It's always been about the job for me. I graduated from college and set out on a sprint to be the best. I didn't have a thing to prove to anyone. I wasn't on a quest to make someone proud. I live for the thrill of taking a company to the next level. I get high from the knowledge that I'm the best at what I do.

I've spent the past year trying to push down my attraction to Lark by spending time with Gem after meeting her at a bar. I wasn't using her at first, but it morphed into that after I realized during a Monday morning marketing meeting months ago that Lark is, without a doubt, unlike any other woman I've ever known. She's beautiful and smart. Her heart is kind and open. It's not tarnished with doubt and regret. She's pure and full of promise.

She was dating a struggling actor who worked at the deli down the street when I had my epiphany, so I took Gem up on her offer when she invited me on a weekend trip to Vegas. She saw it as us taking our relationship to the next level. I saw it as an escape from the knowledge that I may have fucked up my one chance with a woman I felt something real for. I never felt anything for Gem beyond temporary lust and occasional fondness. She gave me an escape, and I gave her a male prop for her pictures. I became a pseudo-celebrity because I was hanging out with a woman who craved fame more than her next breath.

The deli guy was still in the picture a month after I returned from Vegas. I broke up with Gem during that trip, but she wanted me back, so I gave it another chance. It was fun for a few weeks, but that didn't last. In the past two months we slept together less, fought more and then last week when I tagged along on a photo shoot she booked with one of her sponsors in the Caribbean, everything blew apart.

I thought we were on a nude beach, so I stripped because it was too damn hot to wear anything. I have no problem being naked in front of anyone as long as I'm aware and alert. Gem knew we were being photographed. It was her intention for the pictures to go viral. She set me up, and once I realized it after reading an email she left open on her phone, I lost it.

I came back to Manhattan with the intention of swearing off women altogether for the foreseeable future but then I heard that whatever Lark had with the deli guy ended some time ago when he got a bit part in a movie and moved to Los Angeles.

She's still Crew's sister though which means I need to tread lightly, but I want to tread. The work is good. The job is the best I've ever had, but it can't replace what I felt when I kissed Lark.

"Did you just finish a late lunch? What did you have?"

Speak of the devil. I look up from my laptop to see Crew once again in the open doorway of my office. It's nearing six which means the marketing holiday party starts in an hour in the corner boardroom down the hall. I got an update from John when I arrived at the office this morning. The party was moved back a day to accommodate Lark's surprise birthday party.

"Lunch?" I shut the cover of my laptop. "I went to that pub around the corner and had a sandwich hours ago. Why?"

"Something in here smells good." He rubs the bridge of his nose. "Are you wearing new cologne?"

I know the unspoken rule about wearing anything in the office that's not branded by Matiz. I wear the company's cologne and it's not just because I've been given carte blanche to request a complimentary bottle from the store below our offices whenever I want. It's one of the perks of being a senior executive. I wear Matiz cologne because it suits me.

"Not a chance." I smile. "What can I do for you, Crew?"

"Lark was asking questions about you on the way to her party last night."

Questions are good. The fact that he's not flipping the fuck out about it is even better. If I wasn't working for him, I have a sense he'd be okay with me pursuing his sister. I'm three years older than her, established in my career, I rent an apartment on the Upper West Side and I'm a good guy.

"What were the questions specifically?" I ask because he doesn't offer and I'm too curious to drop it.

"She wanted to know if I knew where you'd been fucking off to the last couple of days." He takes one full step forward. He's as aware as I am that John left for the day so no one can overhear our conversation.

"What did you tell her?" My shoulders tense even though I doubt like hell he said a word to Lark about where I was. I know she wanted to talk to me about why I still have the two images of her tattoo on my phone. I saw the question written all over her face the other day when I sent them to her, but I had personal business to take care of, and I'd requested Crew's discretion when I texted him to tell him I wouldn't be in.

"Nothing," he replies with a shrug of his shoulders. "She assumed it was related to Gem. I told her she dumped you and that was the end of it."

"I dumped Gem," I correct him.

"Not according to what she's posting online."

"She's a liar, Crew." I run my hand through my hair. "The worst mistake of my life was hooking up with her. I'll regret that forever."

"Regrets are useless, Ryker. Use that experience as a lesson. You know the kind of woman to stay away from now. Consider yourself lucky that you weren't tied legally to her."

I've thought about that myself. Gem wanted a ring. She begged for one on her birthday a few months ago but I wasn't feeling it. Truthfully, I didn't entertain the thought at all. I want the whole wife and family scene one day, but not with someone like Gem.

"You're too fucking young to worry about shit like this." Crew looks at me with a grin. "You've got years of good hard fun ahead of you before you should even think of settling down. Use me as an example. I'm what… three, four years older than you, and I'm nowhere near ready to hand it over to one woman."

"I'll keep that in mind, Crew. I'll buy you a beer at the party."

"I already bought all the beer for the party and the wine and all the other shit my assistant said she needed for it." He chuckles. "My plan is to tap out now. I don't need to be there. You should show up though. Keep the troops in line."

"They're all looking forward to it." I ease into the subject I've been dying to broach since he showed up. "Is Lark excited for it? I know she had a good time last year."

"Did she?" His mouth curves. "I wouldn't know. I asked about it and she shut me down so I dropped it."

"I'll make an appearance." I stand and extend my hand. "I won't see you again before Christmas break so enjoy the time with your family, Crew."

"You do the same." He gives my hand a firm shake. "You need anything, you call me, Moore. I can round up people to help you out within an hour. If you need the extra hands, I'll make it happen."

I appreciate the offer but I need something else. I need a chance with his sister. I'm hoping tonight I'll get it.

Chapter 10

Lark

"What are you doing over the Christmas break, Lark?" Dexie tips the glass in her hand in my direction. "Are you heading up to Connecticut like you did last year?"

And repeat one of the worst weeks of my life? Nope. I went to Connecticut after my birthday last year with a group of female friends from college. I thought it would be a week filled with shopping, good food and girl talk topped off with a New Year's Eve celebration for the ages. It was none of that. I spent almost an entire week listening to my school friends bitch about the men they'd been dating, the jobs they hated and the gifts they got for Christmas that they didn't want.

"I'm staying home." I take a small sip from the glass of sparkling water in my hand. "I'll clean my closets and organize my kitchen."

"Way to live on the wild side." Christine downs what's left of the wine in her glass. "Dexie and I are going to hit a couple of clubs on New Year's Eve. You're welcome to come with us."

It's a tempting offer but I have other plans for New Year's Eve. My parents own a hotel in Times Square, and they've always kept a suite on the top floor open for anyone who wants to hang out there to watch the ball drop. I've never done it but I've always wanted to and this year seems like the perfect opportunity.

I've done some subtle digging and at the moment, it seems like I'm the only Benton who will be there. I'm good with that. I can welcome next year alone with a clear focus on what I want to accomplish.

"I have plans," I say with conviction. "Thanks for the invite."

"Are your plans with Ryker?" Christine's brows dance. "If they are, can you take pictures? I don't think he would mind. He seems very comfortable in front of the camera."

Dexie laughs but my expression is stoic, my eyes glued to Christine. "Just because he seemed comfortable doesn't mean he was. Those pictures are an invasion of his privacy."

"Look at you defending him again." Christine leans forward. "Are you fucking him? You're fucking Ryker, aren't you?"

"Did you hear what I just said?" I place my plastic wine glass on the conference room table next to where we're standing. "Every time you crack a joke about those pictures, you're disrespecting him."

"I knew something was going on between you two after the way you reacted in the boardroom when I pulled up those memes of his dick." She jabs her index finger into my forearm. "I saw you two kissing by the elevator at the party last year. I thought it was nothing when I heard he was fucking that Instagram model, but you've been his second taste this entire time, haven't you? You give it up to him when she's off jetting around the world. You're his whore on demand."

Her words float around me, but they're so foreign I can't absorb them. "I'm not a whore."

"You kissed him in full view out in that corridor." Her hand flies next to my face in the air. "You were practically sucking his face off, Lark. That's the only reason you're assigned the bigger campaigns. It's because Ryker's dick is so far up your ass, that he can't think straight."

I want to slap her but I can't. My hands shake, my knees tremble but I stand firm. I'm a Benton. My parents taught me to never back down if I'm firm in my conviction. "I'm going to do everything in my power to get you fired."

She laughs so loudly that the sound vibrates off the walls. The room is silent save for the reverberating sound of her cackle. "Good luck with that. I haven't done anything wrong."

"I disagree." Crew steps in place beside me. "You're fired, Christine. As of this second, you no longer work for Matiz."

***

"Ryker kissed you at the Christmas party last year?"

I look up and into Crew's face. I've been sitting at his desk for half an hour. I know I should go back to the party and face my co-workers, but I'm not up to it right now. I don't want to give Christine's ugly accusations any weight. I haven't been granted any special favors by Ryker. I don't have to prove that to anyone.

"I kissed him too." I swallow past the lump in my throat.

"Was that the start of something between you two?" He leans against the edge of his desk.

I don't know how to take that. He's essentially asking me if I was involved with Ryker while he was involved with Gem. My brother knows me so well in many ways and apparently I'm a stranger to him when it comes to where my moral compass is.

"We kissed under the mistletoe and never talked about it. He met Gem. I met Dale from the deli, and we both did our own thing."

"So nothing is going on at the moment between you and Moore?"

"Technically, no," I murmur.

He furrows his brow. "What does that mean?"

His tone is firm, the question expected but infuriating. I shouldn't be required to explain my attraction to my boss to my brother. I'm a grown woman. I don't want to be under his watchful gaze for eternity. "I like him, Crew. I like him a lot."

"You like Ryker?"

My skin peppers with a sheen of nervous sweat. I wore the dress that Crew dubbed as *Mrs. Claus like* tonight and it's clinging to me like a wet second skin. I'm not only uncomfortable because of the topic, but I'm physically uncomfortable too. "I do, yes."

"Because of those pictures that were online?" He rubs his chin. "Is this about those pictures or the kiss?"

"It's about him." I pull on the collar of the dress but it does nothing to offer me a reprieve from the warmth I feel. "I don't even know if he likes me that way, Crew, but I want to find out."

"It's not a good call to get tangled up with someone you work with, Lark. If things hit the rails, you're setting yourself up for a complicated work dynamic with him."

"What if things don't hit the rails, Crew?" I twist my hair into a knot in my hand, exposing my neck to the cool air in his office. "I want to find out for myself. I want to take chances and make mistakes. I want to experience things. I want to know him outside of work."

He studies my face, his eyes narrowing. "You're still my little sister. I don't want your heart to get broken."

I fist my hand on my chest. "I'm not saying I'll fall in love with him, Crew. I just want to see if he feels the same spark that I do."

"I'd never stand in your way." He moves closer, edging the toe of his black oxford against my shoe. "If he made you feel all this from a kiss, take the chance."

"You're not going to flip out when you see him, are you?" I push myself to my feet. "Promise me you won't go all overbearing brother on me if you see me talking to him at the party."

"I can't promise that," he says with a smile. "I can promise to trust that you know what you're doing. He's not at the party, though, Lark."

"He's not?" I pause to collect myself, disappointment rushing through me. "I thought he was going to be there."

"Something came up." He looks at me. "He texted me right before the party started to say he couldn't make it. He asked me to make an appearance in his place."

"Oh." I hear the dejection in my voice. I had pled my case to Crew not only to remove the barrier of his meddling but to convince myself that I needed to take a chance by telling Ryker I'm attracted to him.

Crew lifts his chin. "He asked me to keep this quiet. He trusted me with this, and I don't want to break that."

I want to yank the sister card out of my pocket but I can't. Ryker entrusted my brother with something. If I push to find out more, I'll damage whatever friendship or understanding they've built.

"Is he with a woman?"

"Yes." Crew nods slowly. "It's not what you think though."

"I want to talk to him before anyone else from marketing does. I need to be the one to tell him what Christine said." I fidget on my feet. The sound of the bells on my belt jingling brings an unexpected smile to my mouth. "I guess I should be grateful I won't see him tonight. He'd want nothing to do with me seeing me dressed like this."

"I told you last night that no one can rock a Mrs. Claus look the way you do." He flicks his index finger against the bells. "I think it's the perfect dress to wear to go get some ice cream."

I tilt my head to the side. "Where the hell did that come from? Are you inviting me to go for ice cream with you? It's cold out and you hate ice cream."

"I'm not going." He closes his eyes and arches his neck back. "You should go alone. Go to the place that you always go to. Cremza. Go now."

"You're not setting me up for another surprise party, are you?" I tease. "My heart can't take another one of those."

"There's a surprise waiting for you there, but don't bring my name into it." He taps his finger on my chin. "You got that, sis? I didn't send you there. You're going because you're craving a scoop of mint chocolate chip."

"All right," I manage to say even though I have no idea what's waiting for me at my favorite ice cream shop.

Chapter 11

Ryker

Heaven in a horrid dress just walked into my grandparents' ice cream shop. It's Lark Benton eyeing up the menu and pulling money from her wallet. I watch her in earnest from where I'm standing near a table, clearing away what's left of a banana split for two.

The man and woman, who shared it, fed each other before they practically ran out the door to wherever they're going to next. They might be fucking in the alley next to this place for all I know. Ice cream is apparently an aphrodisiac for some people. It's never been for me. It's too tied to my childhood and summers spent here working behind the counter helping out my mom's folks. I grew up learning the ropes. I took over the business aspect once I graduated from college. The gradual decline of both of my grandparents' memories forced me to take the reins even though I don't draw a paycheck or spend more than a couple of hours a week here.

That changed a few days ago when they both came down with the flu. My mother flew in from Boston to handle the day-to-day, and I've been picking up the slack when I can. I've kept it quiet, wanting to keep a fair distance between the pictures that surfaced online of me last week and the business my family has spent decades building. I can't stomach the thought of their names or Cremza's being drawn into the Gem's self-created public whine fest. She can bitch and moan about me all she wants to her followers or anyone who will listen. I don't want my family to bear the brunt of her scorn.

I've fielded calls on my office phone from Gem's fans who have vowed revenge for upsetting their idol. My social media profiles have been blasted by so many ugly comments that I stopped reading them altogether. I can't stomach the thought of anyone walking in here and subjecting my family to that same treatment all because I'm not with a woman anymore who I should never have been with in the first place.

Time will steal their attention away from me. Gem will post new pictures. She'll find another guy to fuck and I'll go back to being nobody, which is exactly what I want.

"You can't take your eyes off her, Ry." My cousin, Nathan, slaps me on the back. "Is it the dress or the girl?"

"That's her." I don't turn to look at him. "That's the woman I told you about earlier."

"Lark?" He steps in place next to me. "The woman you're crazy for dresses like that?"

I chuckle softly. "She's hot in whatever she's got on. She doesn't put too much out there. She's elegant. She's beautiful, Nate. Just look at her."

"I am. She's a close second to my wife." He pats my shoulder. "Speaking of Jessica, she and the boys are waiting for me at the hotel. I told her I'd stick around here to help you if you need it, but she misses me. She wants me there to tuck the boys in. They're turning in soon because we have an early flight back to Boston in the morning."

Nathan walked through the door unexpectedly two hours ago. He doesn't have any skin in this game. We're connected because our fathers are brothers, yet he showed up to lend a hand. He wanted to pitch in and take on what he could to help me out. He's like a brother to me. I look up to him.

"You're not staying in New York for Christmas?" I finally turn to face him. "I thought you'd stick around."

"It was a two-day trip to spend time with Jessica's sister and her husband." He glances at his watch. "She lives here now. We hung out with them, did some shopping but the family celebration is back in Boston for us. Our roots are there now."

Mine were too once, but New York won me over. I like the energy here. For years I've craved the constant pursuit of trying to prove myself as the best of the best. My internal drive to succeed is here. I doubt I'll ever go back to Boston permanently.

"Don't let her slip through your fingers." Nathan smiles, looking every bit the distinguished attorney he is. "I almost made that mistake with Jessica. You may only get once chance with that girl. Don't fuck it up, Ry."

I turn back to see my mom handing a cone filled with a scoop of chocolate ice cream to Lark. "I won't fuck it up. I'll tell her tonight."

***

"Oh my God," Lark screeches as her single scoop of ice cream hits the floor. "You scared me to death, Mr. Moore."

Mr. Moore.

I need that to end now. It's a turn-on in the office. There's a part of me that enjoys it. I admit I sometimes imagine her on her knees taking my cock down her throat and then thanking me for my release in that sweet voice of hers while she adds a sultry, 'Mr. Moore' to the end of it as she licks her lips.

Jesus. My mom is ten feet away from us and I'm thinking about blowing my load down Lark's throat.

92

"I need you to start calling me
Ryker." I reach for a napkin from the table
she's sitting at and use it to scoop up the ice
cream. "Please call me Ryker, Lark."

She nods. "I can do that. You did
scare me. You can't creep up behind people
like that."

"Do you want another scoop?" I ask
as I toss the ice cream in a waste container
a few feet away. "I'll get you whatever you
want. There's a new bucket of a mint white
chocolate chip in the back. You can be the
first to try it out."

"How do you know that?" She
surveys the almost empty store. Business
isn't as brisk in the dead of winter as it is in
the summer months, but a few new menu
additions my grandmother concocted have
helped. Rich hot chocolate and handmade
baked goods have kept our regulars coming
back regardless of how much snow is on
the ground or how low the temperature
dips. "Do you know the owner?"

"My grandparents own this place." I
lower myself into a wooden chair across
the table from her.

"Your grandparents are Fred and Nellie Albertson?" She rocks back in her chair. "You're not serious?"

"That's my mom behind the counter." I fist my hand in the air, my thumb pointing at the counter behind me. "Her parents founded this place."

"Wow." She bites her bottom lip. "What a small world. They were always telling me that I was perfect for their grandson. Do you have a brother?"

I huff out a laugh. I'm their one and only grandson. "No, Lark. They were talking about me."

Chapter 12

Lark

"I need to ask you something, Ryker." I stand behind him as he locks the door of Cremza. I waited at the table while he closed the shop with his mom. They worked together like a well-oiled machine, moving seamlessly next to one another as they put everything away.

Once they were finished, Ryker introduced me as a co-worker and friend to his mom. She smiled, and her eyes danced as if she was about to burst. Before she could say anything, he kissed her goodbye and hailed her a taxi headed for his grandparents' apartment.

"Are you going to ask me why I smell like cilantro?" He slides the key fob into his jacket pocket.

"You do smell a little like cilantro." I move closer and breathe in his scent. "I just thought you had something delicious to eat for dinner."

"I'll explain the cilantro smell once you ask the question."

I nod, my gaze shifting to the sidewalk next to us. I should ask him back to my place so we can talk in private, but he hasn't mentioned the possibility of us hanging out tonight. I need to gauge his interest before I throw myself at him.

"What's the question, Lark?" He reaches forward to button up my wool coat. "It's getting windy. You should bundle up."

I don't brush his hands away. I like that he's chivalrous. I can tell that he was raised as a gentleman. I've seen it in the office when he's moved back to allow women to step onto the elevator first and when he's held open doors for the female and even the male employees. He has good manners which my mom has always told me is a sure sign of a good heart.

"Why did you keep those pictures of me on your phone?"

His hands stop mid-button. His jaw tightens as he looks into my eyes. "Do you like me, Lark?"

"You're not answering my question."

"Answer mine." His gaze drops to my mouth. "Do you like me?"

"You're a pretty good boss," I half-tease, trying to break the palpable tension between us. "I'd rate you a six on a scale of one-to-ten of good bosses. Ten being the best and one being the worst."

He doesn't crack even the smallest smile. "I'll rephrase for clarity. Do you like me enough to want to fuck me, Lark?"

"You're a ten on that scale."

The corners of his mouth curve up. "I kept the pictures because I want to fuck you. I kept them because I'd look at them and imagine what was underneath your lace panties. I kept those pictures because they were the closest thing I had to this."

There's no time for anything, not a single breath, not a rational thought before he crashes his lips into mine and kisses me the way he did last Christmas.

***

My coat is on the floor within seconds after I shut my apartment door. He claws at me like a wild animal that has finally caught the prey it's been stalking for a lifetime. I reach to help shove his jacket from his shoulders.

"You've seen me nude." He throws his coat onto a chair. "You know what's underneath my clothes. I want to see you."

"It's a chore to get out of this." I wave my hands at my sides. "I had to get my neighbor to zip this up."

"Lucky neighbor." He chuckles as his shirt hits the floor. "I'll unzip it for you. You want this, right? I'm not misreading what's happening here, am I?"

How could he be? We kissed, without stopping once, in the taxi on the way over. I was practically in his lap by the time the driver slowed to a stop next to the curb in front of my building. I fumbled with my keys like an idiot before Ryker took them from my hand and unlocked the door to my apartment.

"Do you have condoms?" I ask in reply to his question. "I don't have any."

"I do," he shoots back with a wide grin. "I have two in my wallet. I'll need to put one on soon. I'm fucking dying here, Lark."

My eyes drop to his hands. He reaches into his wallet, tugging out a foil packet he offers to me. I take it without a word as I watch his hands move to the front of his pants.

He unzips them, pushing them down as he toes out of his shoes. His socks follow and suddenly he's standing before me in nothing more than black boxer briefs.

"I wish this was the first time you were seeing me like this." He hooks his thumbs in the briefs before he pushes them down.

I scan his entire body without any reservation. I don't care that the first time I saw it like this was in a picture on my phone while he stood next to a woman who looked just as flawless as he does nude.

I'm not perfect. I have a small roll around my tummy and my ass isn't as firm as I want, but my body is mine and judging by how hard his cock is, he wants me just as I am.

Chapter 13

Ryker

I slide that fucking ugly dress off her beautiful body before I feather kisses all over her shoulders. I leave her bra and panties on for now because I'm on the brink of coming already. There's a bead of pre-ejaculate on the tip of my cock that I want her to taste, but I don't push. I won't take from her tonight. I'll give if I can last long enough to savor the sweet torture that is her body.

I scoop her up when I kiss her, locking her legs around my waist. I cup her ass in my hand, the barrier of the lace of her black panties taunting me. Her pussy is on fire. I can feel how wet she is through the fabric. I can sense her need because it mirrors my own. It's there in her rapid breaths and the flush of the skin on her neck.

I kiss her as I carry her down the hallway. There's light streaming into the corridor from one of the rooms, so I take my chances and turn there. I see a bed and immediately stalk toward it.

She clings tightly to the condom package I handed her after I took it out of my pocket. She covets it like it's a gift.

She's the fucking gift. This woman's desire for me is the best present I've ever received.

I rest her gently on her back. "If I fuck this up by going too fast, forgive me, Lark. I feel like this is my first time. I want you so much I can't stand it."

She murmurs something under her breath before she reaches to the front of her bra. I push her hands away. I twist the clip and her bra pops open, her plump breasts just inches from my face. I can't resist. I lean down and graze my lips over one tight pale nipple. She squirms with the touch, so I take it between my teeth. I bite just hard enough to bow her back. I lick it then, the gentle lash of my tongue is enough to make her reach up and wind her fingers in my hair.

I've planned this out in my mind a million times. I'd lick her breasts, giving each the attention it deserves before I'd bury my mouth in her pussy. I wanted to taste her and feel her come against my lips before I felt her wrapped around my cock.

I can't wait. The pressure to fuck is too much, so I pull back and kiss her lips again. I have things I want to say, words I need to tell her but it's all buried so deep below my body's own need that I don't say a thing.

I yank the condom package from her and sheath myself quickly. I run my hand over the length of my shaft as her eyes follow my every move.

I grab the edge of her panties. My eyes glued to her body, to the swell of her breasts as her breathing increases both in depth and speed. She tries to help me pull them down, but I shake my head slightly. This is mine. I want this moment to belong to me. I've waited a fucking year for this.

I tug on them and she raises her ass. I slide them down her legs, stopping to kneel to kiss her calf before I toss the panties on the bed.

"Tell me if it feels good, Lark," I coax.

"I like it. I like everything you're doing."

I kiss the top of her pussy. One lick of my tongue over her cleft before I nudge her legs apart. "Don't hold back with me. Tell me how I make you feel. Let yourself go."

She's quiet; a lover so silent that I can only read the subtle nuances in her body's movements to know if I'm giving her what she needs.

She nods. "I will."

I slide my finger over her folds, the sensation pulling a deep groan from the back of my throat. "If I hurt you, you stop me. You'll tell me to stop."

Her back braces against the bed as I graze the tip of my cock over her clit. I could come like this without ever being inside her. The smell of her skin and the fact that she's wet as fuck is enough to send me over the edge. I might die from pure pleasure when I'm inside her. I feel it. She'll grip me so tight I'll feel her pussy wrapped around me for days.

I gasp as I slide the tip in. She whimpers so softly it's barely noticeable. "Let it go, Lark. Let your body feel."

I bury myself completely inside her. My selfish need to consume her is worth the pain that's etched on her beautiful face.

Her hands fist the blanket underneath us, her bottom lip trembles and when I start the fucks at a slow and steady pace, her eyes roll back, her nipples furl into tight points and she finally, finally lets out a barely audible, sweet-as-all-hell moan.

Chapter 14

Lark

"By the way, Christine is fired," I say as I watch him dress. "Crew fired her tonight."

"Why?" he asks without looking at me. "What happened?"

I realize post sex is not the best time to talk business, but I want to have this conversation before someone else texts him to tell him, or he reads about it online on someone's social media account. Christine works for him. I think he values her contributions to the marketing team, but I have no scope of how her termination will impact him or the work he has lined up for us next year.

"She called me a whore." I open with that because in my books worst first is never a bad approach.

"Christine called you a whore?" He finally looks at me. "You're the farthest thing from a whore. What the fuck is wrong with her?"

"She started talking about your dick pics when we were at the party." I sigh. "I told her to stop and she said she saw us kissing last year and that I was your whore on the side. She said when you weren't fucking Gem you were fucking me."

"Jesus Christ." He wraps his arms around me, tugging me closer to him. "You had to listen to that? I'm sorry, Lark. I'm sorry I wasn't there."

"I was handling it," I say as I lean my cheek against his chest. "Then Crew stepped in and dropped the gauntlet. He was furious. He heard everything she said."

"He heard it all?" He pushes me back so he can look down at my face. "He must be pissed."

"He's mad at Christine." I roll my eyes. "She wasn't quiet when she was on her rant. Every person in the room heard it."

"They heard her say that she saw us kissing?"

"Yes." I suck in a deep breath.

"Crew knows that we kissed?" He winces as if he's being punched in the gut. "Do I still have a job to go back to?"

I pat him playfully on his chest. "Crew has his reservations about us, but your job isn't in jeopardy. He trusts me to do what I want and to handle things if this doesn't work out."

Confusion etches his brow. "You and Crew discussed the two of us before you came to Cremza tonight?"

I don't want to lie to Ryker about what brought me to Cremza, but I owe Crew for pointing me in his direction. "We talked about you and the kiss we shared last year. I left the office after that and came to Cremza to get an ice cream."

"He's okay with the fact that we kissed last year?"

"He is." I smile. "I'm not going to fill him in on what we did tonight. Some things are better kept behind closed doors."

"I agree." He slips his coat back on. "I asked him not to mention to anyone that my family owns Cremza and that I've been helping out there. Gem's fans have been relentless with their attacks on me. I wanted to keep Cremza out of it, so I thought the fewer people who know the better but I'm glad he told you where to find me."

"Me too."

"I need to run, Lark. I have some work at Matiz I have to finish up before the break. I didn't have a chance to get to it this week so I have to clear it off my desk tonight."

I'd offer to tag along and help, but it's an offer he could have made if he wanted to. He didn't so I'm staying put inside my warm apartment. "I understand."

"I'll be busy with family stuff over the next few days. I'll call you on your birthday."

It's a sweet gesture. I want to ask him to stay but he's already got one foot out the door, literally. The door to my apartment is open and his left foot is in the corridor.

"I'd like that," I say quietly.

He reaches into his pocket and tugs something out.

I laugh aloud when I catch sight of it. "You had that in your pocket, Ryker? Why?"

He holds it in the air above my head. It's a small bunch of wilting cilantro. The stems are wrapped in red ribbon and tied in a bow. "I wanted a repeat of last year. This was my guarantee to get it."

"I didn't think you remembered that kiss."

"I'll never forget that kiss." He leans forward and softly brushes his lips over mine. "I let you walk away after I kissed you then. I'm not going to make that same mistake twice."

"Why did you act like it never happened?" I try to form a smile. "For an entire year I thought you completely forgot about it."

He cups my chin in his hand. "You'd barely look at me after that. I thought you regretted it. I knew it could complicate things at work for both of us so I didn't bring it up again."

"What's changed now?" I question, pinning my gaze to his. "What makes this year different than last?"

"I've spent too long trying to run from what I feel for you." His thumb traces a circle on my skin. "I'm tired of running. I want you. I'm not waiting another year to make sure you know it."

"What about Gem?" I blurt out the question without considering how it tarnishes the moment.

"What about the guy from the deli? I couldn't order one of my favorite sandwiches for months because I couldn't stand the sight of him. I knew you were kissing him, touching him. I knew he was important to you."

I take a step back. "He's nothing to me. It was a fling. He was a distraction."

"Gem was the same." He closes the distance between us. "They're both in the past. They need to stay there."

"I agree." I scrub my hand over my face.

"You want to talk about Gem and why I was with her, don't you? You want me to explain why I started anything with her when I'd just kissed you? Is that what you want, Lark?"

It is. I want all of that. I want him to tell me why tonight couldn't have happened a year ago. I want to know why I wasted so many nights with Dale while I constantly thought about him with Gem.

"Was my kiss not enough?" I ask sheepishly.

"It was too much." He presses his lips to my temple. "I was confused by it, terrified as fuck. I wanted the job more than anything back then and your brother was scary as hell when I first started at Matiz. I knew if I pursued you, it would potentially complicate my position and work has always been everything to me. I found Gem and tried to forget our kiss."

"Would you take Gem back if she came here for you?"

"Never." He closes his eyes. "I left her for good, Lark. That woman is nothing to me. Don't let her ruin tonight."

"She left you," I correct him. "I might be a rebound. Am I a rebound?"

"I left her. I hadn't slept with Gem in months." He looks me square in the eyes. "We didn't sleep together in the Caribbean. I can't remember the last time I touched her. We were in a relationship without an anchor."

"Why did you go on that trip with her?"

"One of her swimsuit sponsors offered her a companion ticket and I bummed along because she had no one else to go with. I hadn't used my vacation days for this year and I was just about to lose them. We were friendly, not friends, but friendly enough that I tagged along."

"Do you strip like that in front of all your friends?"

"It was too hot out that day. I'm from the northeast, Lark. I can't handle that heat so I stripped. She did the same. She'd seen me naked enough times that I didn't think twice about it. If you hadn't noticed, I wasn't hard in those pictures. Her body did nothing for me at that point."

I didn't expect to have this conversation with him tonight, but then again, I didn't expect us to end up in my bed either. I sound like I think we are in a relationship when all we did was fuck.

"I'm usually not this curious after I've slept with a man." I attempt a laugh. "I must sound insane to you. I was just wondering about Gem."

"You shared your body with me tonight." He kisses the top of my hand. "You have the right to ask me anything."

"Thank you."

"I'm going to sprint." He takes another step out the door, his eyes raking over the white robe I'm wearing. "I can see your nipples through that, Lark. Lock the door when I leave. I don't trust any of your neighbors to stay away from you."

I laugh as I watch him jog down the corridor before he pushes open the door that leads to the stairs.

Chapter 15

Lark

"All you wanted for Christmas was a bang from your boss and boy, did he deliver."

I snap my head up to look at Isla standing in front of me. "I thought you were putting Ella to bed. Where is Gabriel? I don't want him to hear you talking about my sex life."

"With any luck, he's getting the swing ready for his Christmas gift later."

I cover my face with my hands. "You and Gabriel do not do all those kinky things you say you do."

"After you leave tonight, my husband is going to strap me to the sex swing that he had installed in the extra bedroom, and he's going to fuck me good and hard until I beg him to stop."

Since I can't tell if she's serious or not, I change the subject. "Thank you for the cake and the gift, Isla. I love the scarf."

She eyes the plaid scarf she gave me earlier. "It's beautiful. I saw it in October and I thought it would look perfect on you. I picked it up then and wrapped it."

"You wrapped it in birthday gift wrap," I note. "You didn't use Christmas wrapping paper."

"It's a birthday gift, Lark." She smooths her hand over the back of my hair. "We exchange birthday gifts."

I like the subtle distinction. As much as I've complained about being born on Christmas Day, I've always felt joy in it as well. I may not have the distinction of having a day all to myself, but I've never celebrated a birthday without my family surrounding me. That happened earlier when I spent the afternoon and early evening with my folks and my brothers.

"Did Ryker call you today?" She leans forward and presses her finger on my phone's home button.

I glance down at where it's resting on the dining room table. "No, and he didn't text me either."

She points at the digital clock." There are less than two hours left until your birthday is officially over."

I know. I've been watching the clock carefully since I left my parents' condo to come to Isla and Gabriel's apartment for cake and ice cream. I expected to hear from Ryker on my birthday, mainly because he said I would.

This morning, during a brief text message exchange, before she opened gifts with her family, I'd filled Isla in on almost everything that happened between Ryker and me the night of the party at Matiz.

"I drilled him with questions about his ex before he left my place the other night," I admit with a sigh. "That might have been enough to scare him off."

"Maybe." She sits down in the chair next to me. "If it was, he's not the guy for you."

He is the guy for me. I feel it. It's not just the great sex talking. It's everything. It's the way his lips feel against mine and how my pulse races when he looks into my eyes.

"You should text him." She picks up my phone and drops it in my lap. "Text him and ask him to meet you for a birthday drink."

"No." I laugh off the suggestion. "I'm not going to come off like that woman."

"What woman?"

"The one who is so desperate to hear from the guy she slept with that she tracks him down."

"You read too many advice columns." She reaches to pull the dish of ice cream she was eating earlier closer to her. "If you want to talk to him, call him. He's not going to think you're desperate, Lark. He'll think you like him."

***

I cross the street and head straight for Rockefeller Centre. I was just about to take Isla's advice to send Ryker a text to wish him a Merry Christmas but he beat me to it with a call. He asked me to meet him in front of the enormous tree that New Yorkers and tourists alike flock to every year. I always manage a quick visit to the tree every December. I did that last week when snow was lightly falling. I stood and stared at it before I walked back up to Broadway and took an Uber to my place.

"Lark," he calls to me with a wave of his hand. "I'm over here."

I try not to run although I want nothing more than to jump into his arms. His hair is messy, evidence of the wind that rose up right after dinner. He's dressed casually in jeans and the same black wool coat he wore the night he came to my place.

"Happy Birthday." He skims his tongue over his bottom lip before he kisses me softly. "I made it just in time, didn't I?"

I think he did. I haven't checked the time since I heard back from him. "It's good to see you, Ryker. Merry Christmas."

"It's great to see you. I would have called sooner but I've had a shit day. One of the freezers at Cremza failed. I finally got that sorted when I found a repair guy who wasn't after my firstborn in exchange for a fix." He exhales in a rush. "I got you something. I picked it up yesterday. I didn't have time to wrap it or anything but I wanted to give it to you now, here in front of the tree."

I look up at the colorful lights. Only a few people are milling about, most of them focused on capturing a selfie in front of the tree. "It's a perfect spot. Is it more cilantro?"

"You'll kiss me without that, won't you?" He reaches to squeeze my chin. "You can't expect me to walk around forever smelling like that."

Forever.

One word with a lifetime of meaning.

"I like the way you smell today." I step closer to him.

"I'll like the way I smell later." He closes the small bit of distance left between us. "I'll smell like you. Your smell will be all over my face."

I smile at the promise of what's to come. Me, specifically if he has his way.

"Close your eyes and open your palms, Lark." He gently slides his fingers over my eyes. "I'll put your surprise in your hands."

I do as I'm told, even though I can feel my hand shaking in anticipation.

I hear the music before I feel the weight of the gift. The song is haunting and beautiful. It's familiar to everyone, yet special to me.

"Open your eyes," he whispers against my cheek.

I do. I look down at the snow globe in my hands. It's a scene that matches the one we're standing in the middle of. There's a tree with the Rockefeller Centre behind it. Spots of colored paint mimic the lights. He must have shaken it before he gave it to me because the snow within is gently falling. It's punctuated by the ongoing melody of Silent Night in the background.

"I love snow globes." I stare at it. "This one is perfect."

"Last week I overheard you telling Dexie that you were coming here to see the tree because you do that every year."

"You were eavesdropping?" I don't look up.

"Yes." He picks up the globe and shakes it again, so the snow rains down. "I saw the snow globes lined up on the windowsill in your bedroom the other night. I could tell that you like them."

"I love them." I finally look up at him.

"You love Silent Night too." His gaze is soft on my face. "You hum it all day at the office. I love the sound. I love the song now too."

I hold the snow globe tightly in my hands. "My mom used to sing it to me every Christmas night before I fell asleep."

"I'll sing it to you tonight."

I feel my eyes well with tears. "You'd do that for me?"

"I'd do anything for you, Lark. Anything."

Chapter 16

Ryker

Sweat runs down my temple. I brush it away with a quick swipe of my hand. I'm not moving. I don't care how hot it is in this room. I'm a man on a mission, and right now my goal is to coax another orgasm out of Lark.

I ate her pussy once while she quietly circled her hips and tugged on my hair. I took her silence to mean I wasn't doing a good enough job even though she flooded my tongue with the tangy taste of her release when she fell over the edge.

I know she's fighting her desire to scream and cry out.

"You don't have to be shy with me, Lark." I kiss the inside of her thigh, my lips stalling over her small heart-shaped tattoo. "You can be as loud as you want."

"My neighbors," she whispers. "I don't want them to know what we're doing."

"They can't hear us." I jerk my head toward the radiator. "That fucking thing sounds like a freight train. It's like Grand Central in here. No one can hear you come but me."

"The super will fix the heat issue in a few days." She skims her hand over her belly and the hint of sweat that's coating her skin. "We can stop if it's too hot for you."

I crawl up her nude body, pressing my erection against her stomach before I straddle her. "I'm not stopping. I want to drink in the taste of you. I want that to be what's on my tongue when I wake up tomorrow."

She swallows hard. "You're different than other men."

"I sure as hell hope so." I chuckle as I push my hair back from my forehead.

"No." She shakes her head, causing a few strands of her long blonde hair to stick to the side of her face. "You touch me in different ways. You kiss me in places I'm not used to. You want me to be loud."

If that was her first time receiving oral I fucked it up. I didn't give it my all. I intend to but that was just a prelude of what's to come.

"Was that your first time, Lark?" I ask even though I'm not sure she'll answer. "Have you never been eaten out before?"

She covers her face with her hands. "I have. My first boyfriend did it, but not like you do. You kiss me there like you kiss my mouth."

I yank her hands into mine, pinning them next to her head on the bed. "Your pussy is as delicious as your mouth. I'll salivate every time I think about it now. I'll want to taste it every time we're together."

"You don't mean that." She tries to laugh my comments away.

"I mean every word." I dip my head to circle her right nipple with my tongue. "I'm going to savor you the way you deserve. I'm going to help you experience everything you want."

"I've had experiences." A pink blush blooms on her cheeks. "I've had lovers."

"You've had sex partners," I correct her. "You've never had a lover. A lover would worship all of this. He'd crave it and beg you for more when you're ready to fall asleep."

She studies my face intently.

"A lover would need to hear you come as much as he feels it. He'd want you to yearn for his touch as much as he yearns for yours. He'd make love to you tenderly and then flip you over and fuck you hard. When he's done, a lover will hold you and remind you that he'll never fucking get enough of you."

Her eyes skim over my body. "Are you my lover?"

I rest my forehead against hers. "Absolutely. I'm your lover. You're only lover and you're mine."

***

I got what I wanted for Christmas. The second time I skimmed my tongue over her clit, she cried out. It was brief and before the orgasm consumed her, her hand was over her mouth sheltering the sounds.

I'd rolled a condom over my cock right after as the taste of her lingered on my tongue. I was relentless, driving my dick into from behind so her so hard the headboard pounded out a rhythmic beat on the wall. That's when she gave me the most precious gift she could have. She moaned as she climaxed. It was music to my ears and enough to make me come. I did. It was so intense that it dropped me to my knees beside the bed when I tried to stand.

I'd found just enough strength after that to toss the condom into the wastebasket before I crawled into bed with her.

"Do you have to go?" She pushes her naked back into my chest.

"No." I wrap my arms around her. "I'm staying. I don't need to be anywhere until tomorrow afternoon."

"We can fall asleep like this," she whispers. "I'll sleep like a baby tonight."

I will too but first I have to do something. I lean forward and cocoon myself around her. Then I rest my lips against her ear and I softly sing Silent Night to my Christmas angel.

Chapter 17

Lark

I wake to silence. There's no sound in the room, only the distant blast of a car horn from somewhere outside the closed window. The radiator quieted sometime during the night which means my bedroom is cold. It's too cold. I slide my legs over the cooled sheet; the bite of the chill of the air entices me to tug the blanket closer, wrapping it around my body. I open my eyes then, wanting to see his handsome face next to me.

The indentation of where his head met the pillow is all that's there. The blanket is flung open on his side. The sheet is still warm from where his large frame was.

"Ryker," I call out quietly. "Where are you?"

My gaze catches on the empty nightstand. I saw his phone there during the night when I woke briefly to pinch myself to make sure it was all real. We'd make love before he sang me to sleep with a raspy and soothing version of my favorite Christmas song.

I must have slept for an hour or two before his hands were on me again. I'd taken the lead buoyed by his words last night about lovers and needs. I took his cock in my mouth and let my desire for him take over. I'd licked and sucked, not caring if I was doing everything right. I moaned around his cock when it touched the back of my throat.

He liked that. His hands twisted in my hair, his hips bucked.

I braced myself to take his come but he'd pulled back and stumbled into the other room. He came back with a condom and slid on top of me, fucking me slowly while I clung to him, riding the crest of my orgasm over his.

I whispered in his ear then that Boyd, the first man I gave myself too, laughed when I let myself go. I'd chanted *'Oh God'* over and over as I rode his cock and Boyd the bastard had stalled, stilling me with his hands on my hips. He'd laughed at me before he told me that I sounded like a hyena.

The words haunted me, guiding my voice whenever I was with a man until last night.

Ryker kissed me when I confessed to him that he made me feel safe.

"Ryker?" I call out again, louder this time. "Are you in the washroom?"

Silence is the only response, so I tug the blanket free and wrap it around me like a cocoon.

I trudge through my apartment, ducking my head in the bathroom before I scan the kitchen. His clothes are gone, just as his phone is.

I stalk to the window and look down on the street. The sidewalk is covered in a blanket of thick fluffy snow. It's still falling. The white gold is a treasure to New Yorkers like me who wait for those few brief days a year when nature slows the city.

I stare at the large flakes and the people walking past my building.

I search for my phone finally finding it at the bottom of my purse. I tug it out and wipe the sleep from my eyes before I call his number.

It rings again and again until his voicemail finally picks up. I hang up without leaving a message.

I send him a text message then, asking him where he ran off to. I try to keep the tone light. I type it out three times and delete it twice before I finally send it.

I cradle the phone in my hands while I wait but there's nothing. Minutes pass, first ten and then fifteen. The silence tempts my curiosity.

I open the browser on my phone and type in Ryker's name in the search bar.

His corporate profile at Matiz pops up and his social media accounts. I scroll through those, most of them a tribute to his job and his love of the outdoors. There are pictures of him hiking and fishing last summer. A few of him are with two men his age who must be his friends.

I'm back to the search function again, and I type in her name. It's just her first name because that's all it takes. Gem.

Her Instagram page is the first result and as my thumb hovers over the link, my stomach clenches but I click it anyway. I click it because I want the reassurance that her picture won't bother me anymore. I want to know that I can look at her and not feel the twinge of jealousy I used to.

That's not what I feel when I scan the most recent picture at the top of the page.

I feel like a fucking idiot.

Ryker, with a shadow of a beard covering his jaw, is in the very first picture I see. I click on it. It was posted sixteen minutes ago at a diner two blocks from here. He's sitting on a leather bench next to a table with a cup of coffee in front of him, and a container of cream to the side. He's wearing the same black wool coat he was last night and his hair looks exactly as it did before he fell asleep in my arms.

He's not looking at the camera. His head is tilted slightly; his eyes cast down.

I read the caption. Once and then again before I leave my phone by the window and walk back to my bedroom, the words Gem posted suffocating me from the inside out.

My boy is back and our future is bright.

Chapter 18

Ryker

"You didn't post a fucking picture of me, did you?" I seethe. "I told you no pictures, Gem. I meant it."

She shakes her head. "Calm down, Ry."

I pick up my phone and immediately open the browser. I search for her name because I've cleared my history of all links to every single social media account she has. I open the first link. "Jesus. *My boy is back and our future is bright?*' That's bullshit. I'm not back. We don't have a future. Delete it."

"I need you, Ryker." She doesn't pick up her goddamn phone to delete the picture of me. "My fan engagement has dropped by thirty percent since I stopped posting about you. People have noticed that you deleted all the pictures of me from your Instagram."

It was one fucking picture taken at a concert three months ago. I never wanted whatever we had to be official in any capacity. "Take down the goddamn picture, Gem."

"No." She pushes her phone away from her. "You're ruining things for me, Ryker. You know I'm close to signing a deal for a reality show. The producer will only do it if you're part of it. He wants the friction between us. He says it's good television."

"I came down here because you texted me forty-five fucking times in the past two days." I tap my finger on the coffee-stained white table between us. "I don't know how the hell you found out about Cremza but that final text you sent last night was the end of it. If you go there and speak to either of my grandparents, I will ruin you, Gem. I will post pictures of you without all that shit you wear on your face."

I'm bluffing. If I took a picture of Gem, I usually deleted it within days. I had no reason to save a picture of her. She put enough of herself out into the world that her pictures feel like worthless currency now. If I ever felt the urge to gaze at a picture of her while we were together, I could just go online. I rarely did.

"You wouldn't," she screeches like I just threatened to lock her up and throw away the key. "That would destroy my career."

"Career?" I toss the word back with a smirk. "You don't have a career."

"You've never understood what I do."

"I never wanted to," I respond calmly. "We were never good for each other, Gem. I need you to take down that picture of me you just posted and I then I want you to fuck off."

She laughs. "You need to step off the merry-go-round, Ryker. We do this again and again, around and around we go. You know it's just a matter of time before we're back together. Don't prolong this. I want you back today. "

I study her face. I don't know what I ever saw in her. She's attractive in an abstract way. Brown hair, blue eyes and a body that's been touched by a plastic surgeon or two. I liked her best when she didn't wear makeup and her phone was out of her hand but once her online profiles caught steam, her obsession with her fan base grew. I was a prop in her picture perfect world. It was never about me after she gained notoriety.

It was always a shallow escape from what I thought I could never have. I thought Lark was out of my reach so I settled.

"I'm done with being part of your circus." I pick up her phone. "Delete the picture you posted and the one you sent me this morning that you took of me inside Cremza. I want out of your world, Gem. I'm not playing the game anymore. I'm finished and this time it's for good."

"If I delete all those pictures, you'll delete the bad ones you took of me?" She takes her phone from me. "I'll leave you alone if you promise to trash the images of me without makeup and the ones you took when I was bloated after that dinner we had in the West Village. I hate that picture. It could wipe out my career just like that if it ever got out."

I stifle back a laugh. How I was ever attracted to her is beyond me. "You've got yourself a deal, Gem."

***

"Lark?" I almost run right into her as I exit the diner. "What are you doing here?"

"You weren't in bed when I woke up." She looks past me, her gaze skimming over the windows.

Gem is still in there, crafting a post about how she dumped my ass for good. I don't give a shit. She can say what she wants about me. I know the truth. If Lark knows, that's all that matters.

"You were sound asleep so I didn't want to wake you." I adjust the scarf that's around her neck. "You read my note, right? I told you I'd be back within the hour."

"I didn't see it at first." Her bottom lip trembles. "You left it next to my pillow. I saw it when I walked back into my bedroom after checking my phone."

"You shouldn't have come out in the cold. It's snowing," I point out the obvious. "You're not dressed very warmly."

"Did you mean what you wrote in the note?"

I wrap my arm around her shoulder and guide her to the side of the building. I know she's not talking about the part of the note where I wrote about which diner I was going to meet Gem at so I could put a stop to her constant harassment. Lark is talking about the rest of the note. She's referring to the words I wrote about her. "I meant every word."

She stops and looks up at me. "Last night was the best night of your life?"

"Until tonight when you let me stay with you again." I rub the tip of her reddened nose. "Then tomorrow night will be better and the next night will be the best."

"You called me your Christmas angel in the note." Her eyes well with tears. "Is that what I am?"

"You're my everyday angel. I want to spend every day with you, Lark. Today, tomorrow, New Year's Eve. All of next year. All of it."

"It's fast. You just broke up with her last week."

"My heart was never attached to her," I say honestly. "I've felt more in the past few days than I've ever felt in my life."

"Me too." She sighs. "We'll take it slow, right? These things need time to grow. We can't rush this. I don't want this to crash and burn."

"We won't crash and burn. This right here is just the beginning of us."

Chapter 19

7 Weeks Later

Ryker

"I'm proud of you, Ryker. I think you're doing the right thing."

"Is that excitement I hear in your voice, Lark?" I look down at her. "You want my job while I'm gone, don't you? Is that why you blew my mind this morning?"

"I blew your dick." She nods, her lips pursing. "I did it because I like you, not because I want your job. Besides, Crew is too controlling to let you pick who covers for you. He'll make that decision himself."

She's right. Her brother is the man with the plan. I spoke to him this morning about my need to take a leave of absence to get things in order at Cremza. I expect to be gone for six weeks while I help my grandparents hire someone to take over the everyday duties of managing the business. I'll still have the upper hand when it comes to all decisions and I'll keep a close eye on things once I'm back at Matiz, but I need to devote time to helping them transition into being semi-retired. It's a decision they made in early January when they realized that there are things they want to do but haven't had the time for.

"You'd make an excellent replacement." I tease her bottom lip with the pad of my thumb. It's the same lip that held the last lingering drops of my release after I'd come down her throat this morning. I didn't expect it, never imagined that she'd blow me in the kitchen of my apartment after we'd shared a bowl of cereal together.

The orgasm was fulfilling, the sounds she made after I picked her up, knocked the bowl into the skin and then ate her out was my heaven. She's given in and opened up. She no longer hears the words of her first piece of shit boyfriend who didn't understand that the cries of a woman under your touch are the fuel most men crave. He was a bastard who took something from her but she's taken it back now. She's free to be herself.

She's given me more these past six weeks than any man deserves.

"It's Valentine's Day tomorrow. What do you want to do?" She has a half-assed grin on her face. "Do you even do Valentine's Day? You seem like you would."

"I don't," I answer truthfully. I've never been one of those guys who trudge down to the store to pick up a heart-shaped box of chocolates or a greeting card with a generic message. I've never done anything for any woman on that day. If I had, it would have been epic. It will be epic this year.

Disappointment wells in her eyes, but her expression holds firm. She's never asked me for a thing since we started seeing each other. Our connection has grown at its own pace. I'm falling in love with her, not just because of who she is when we're alone together but because of the incredible person she is at the office. She holds her own, every single day.

She didn't expect Crew or me to clean up the mess Christine made in the office.

Once the holiday break was over, Lark called a meeting. She explained what everyone had overheard Christine saying and then she told them that we were involved. She was straightforward when she backed it up with a promise to keep everything personal outside of the office. She's done that. I've treated her as much like every other employee as I can. I haven't granted her any special treatment. I've given her the task of heading the marketing campaign for a new women's fragrance we're launching in the fall. Her ideas are brilliant, and her talent is undeniable. She wants to be a part of the team and I'm the captain for now. That may change one day, but we both respect the job when we're at the office. Matiz comes first until we're alone.

She'll contribute to the holiday campaign, but she won't take the lead this year. She's good with that. She understands that I need her to focus more fully on the fragrance and she's eager to head the launch.

"Maybe we can order in pizza?" she asks dejectedly. "Or something else. We'll see what we feel like having tomorrow night."

"I'll be at Cremza until late tomorrow night, Lark. If you want to drop by, I'll buy you a scoop of your favorite for Valentine's Day."

She looks at me like I'm a fucking jerk. Who invites their girlfriend to an ice cream shop for a free scoop on the most romantic day of the year?

"You don't pay for the ice cream there," she points out. "I guess I can come by for a few minutes after work."

"I'll be waiting for you," I say as I pull her close to me, hoping she can't hear how hard my heart is beating. I will be waiting for her with a gift I had made just for her.

Chapter 20

Ryker

I wanted to make love to her last night, but she blew me off and not in a good way. She went to bed early when Nathan called to check in. He's the only person I've told about the surprise I have planned for Lark. I needed his opinion, and I got it. He approved. He told me I was making him proud so I took that as a sign to go full steam ahead.

I left her apartment before her this morning. I kissed her tenderly and wished her a great day. She had pouted with that fucking adorable mouth of hers before she told me she wanted me to have a fantastic Valentine's Day. I smacked her ass and wished her the same and then left as her mouth was hanging wide open.

Now, I'm standing at the door of Cremza and looking out onto the street. Cars pass by. People dodge each other as they scramble to get where they're going on the sidewalk. Everyone has a place they need to be. I know where my place is. It's with Lark.

I see her as she crosses against the light. Her hand in the air as if that will yield off any traffic racing toward her. She's dressed in that black wool coat she's always wearing and red mittens, a red scarf and there's the hint of a red dress swaying around her legs as she walks.

I open the door as she nears.

"Ryker." She stares me down. Her eyes run over the charcoal sweater and black pants I'm wearing. "You look extra nice. You usually wear jeans and a T-shirt when you're here."

I do, but not today.

"Come inside." I tug on her hand. "It's cold outside."

She steps over the threshold of the door and freezes in place. "What is this? What's going on?"

"Take off your coat."

She does. She slips each button from its hole before I help slide it from her shoulders. I fold it carefully and place it on the back of a chair. Then I turn and lock the door.

"You did this for me, Ryker? This is all for me?"

It's nothing. A few white lights strung from the ceiling, soft music, a fuck ton of white and red roses in those glass jars she loves. There's an envelope too and a gift wrapped in red paper.

"Happy Valentine's Day, baby." I rest my cheek against hers as I embrace her from behind. "This is my first Valentine's Day so be gentle."

"I got you something." She spins around quickly, her hands darting to my shoulders. "I got you a gift. It's not extravagant because we hadn't talked about Valentine's Day, so I wasn't sure if a gift was a good idea."

"Do you have it with you? Show me."

"Someone's eager." She laughs as she points at her purse. "I wrapped it after you left this morning. It's in there."

I arch my brow. "Can I open it?"

"Yes," she says patiently, leaning forward to sweep her lips along the stubble that's settled over my jawline. "This is the perfect place for you to open it. We've been coming here together so often since Christmas. I love it here. I love talking to your grandparents and your mom when she's in town. I know I always tell you but I'll never forget New Year's Eve. Seeing your grandparents watching the ball drop was an experience I'll remember for the rest of my life. They both mean a lot to me."

She means a lot to them too. It was her idea to invite my grandparents to the hotel her family owns on New Year's Eve. Both my grandparents had tears in their eyes when they stood by the window and watched the ball drop. It was a bird's eye view of the city they love celebrating a new beginning. Lark had opened one of the windows just enough let the sounds in, but keep the cold out. We toasted with cider at midnight and as my granddad kissed my grandmother, I kissed Lark. It was a night I'll never forget either.

I open her bag and spot the gift right away. It's a rectangular box wrapped in white paper with a red ribbon and bow. "Do you want to open your gift first, baby?"

"No." She shakes her head. "I'm so nervous, Ryker. Please just open it."

I do. I rip it open quickly, the paper flying in the air, ribbon dangling from my fingers. I pull the lid off the box and smile immediately. Fuck. Just fuck. This woman is everything.

"Nellie told me that when you used to work here when you were a teenager that you insisted on having your own ice cream scoop. She said you wouldn't let anyone else touch it. You carved your name in the handle."

Her red-tipped fingernail runs over the smooth wood of the handle of the ice cream scoop and my name etched out by my own teenage hand in uneven lettering.

"Where did you get this, Lark?"

She looks up at me, her gray eyes locked on my face. "Your grandmother kept it in a box in the back. When she told me the story about the scoop on New Year's Eve, I asked if she still had it. Last week I asked one of the drivers that Crew uses to pick me up so I could pick up Nellie and bring her here. We spent a couple of hours in the back going through the boxes until I found it."

She did that for me? She dug into my past to find something that no one would see as meaningful but me. The scoop was part of my identity here. It was a symbol of the hard work and dedication that my grandparents instilled in me. I thought it was gone. I'd broken the handle one afternoon and the next day when I went to pick up the scoop from the drawer behind the counter it was gone. "Where was I when you two were on this treasure hunt?"

"At Matiz. You were in a meeting with Crew."

"That bullshit meeting? The one where he talked about pizza and beer for almost two hours?"

"That's the one. I asked him to keep you busy."

"The handle was cracked and the metal tarnished so I had it fixed up so you can use it again now when you work the counter."

I kiss her with a need I haven't felt before. I love her. I fucking love Lark Benton more than I love anything in this world.

"Thank you, baby," I whisper against the smooth skin of her cheek. "I love it."

"Good," she replies softly. "I want you to love everything I give you."

"Let me give you something now." I take her by the hand leading her to the counter and the gift that I had made for her.

She eyes the envelope. "What's that?"

"You'll open that after you open this." I pick up the box and hand it to her.

"It's heavy." She furrows her brow. "Is it a book? Did you buy me that new Nicholas Wolf novel?"

She's recently fallen in love with his work. She bought herself every book he's ever written in early January. She brought one of the books to my place with the intention of reading it each night before she fell asleep. I never let her have the chance. I'd take her after she crawled into bed, giving her the pleasure I know she craves and taking mine from her. The book was a permanent fixture in my apartment for weeks before she finally took it to her apartment to read during the nights she stayed there.

I started tracking his release schedule then and when he announced he was doing a book signing in Times Square a few weeks ago to celebrate his latest book, I stood in the freezing cold in a long-ass line to get a copy signed personally for her. I told Crew about it and that's when he decided to share the fact that he knows the guy. They went to high school together so the next time he releases anything, I have Crew's word that he'll get me a signed copy.

The copy I did get signed is wrapped and waiting for her on the bed in my apartment.

"It's not a book, Lark."

"Is it a brick?"

I try not to let my anxiety show.
I've never gotten a woman a gift before,
other than my mom or grandmothers. It
was always easy with them. This was
different. I didn't have a lot of time when I
picked out Lark's birthday gift, but this
time I had weeks. I planned this, found
someone to help me bring it to life and now
I'm about to see her reaction. "Lark, I need
you to open it now. Please just open it."

She nods. "All right. I'll love it,
Ryker. Whatever it is, I'm going to love it."

She places the box back on the
counter before she carefully pulls on the
corner of the ribbon. I want to rip the
wrapping paper off of it and pull the box
open, but it's her gift. I bite on the nail of
my thumb while I tap the toe of my shoe on
the floor.

Her heels rise as she stands on her
tiptoes and peers into the open box. A
piece of red tissue paper flies out and then
her hands dart to her mouth. "Ryker, it's
beautiful."

It is. I thought the same and I'm no judge. I didn't look to anyone for guidance, so I've been running on hope. I need this to take her breath away. I want her to understand where my heart is and this is the way to do it.

She reaches into the box and tugs. The snow globe comes free of all the tissue paper it's nestled in. She places it gently on the counter before she bends slightly to look at it directly.

I pick it up to wind up the music box. Silent Night plays softly from it. I start talking because I can't fucking keep quiet. I need to explain so she'll understand the true intention of the gift.

"That's me and you in there, baby. You're wearing that Christmas dress you like. You know the ugly one with the plaid pattern. I'm wearing my best suit. It's that black one you love."

She tilts her head, her eyes pinned to the globe.

"That's the tree in Rockefeller Centre. I know how much you love that tree."

She looks up and into my face, tears masking her beautiful eyes. "You're on your knee, Ryker. You're holding a tiny box with a…"

"It's small but that's a diamond ring."

"An engagement ring?" She looks at the globe before her gaze moves back to me. "Are you going to ask me to marry you?"

"On your birthday." I reach for her hands and feather kisses over the back of them. "When I told you on New Year's Eve that this was our year, I meant it. I know it's too soon to ask you to marry me today but your birthday is perfect. You'll wear the dress, and I'll wear the suit and we'll go to the tree."

"I'll say yes."

I swallow hard. "I want to ask now, Lark."

"I want you to do it on my birthday." She shakes the globe and snow falls over the scene. "I want this to be our engagement. I want you to ask me to be your wife on Christmas Day."

"It's a date." I kiss her softly. "You can open the envelope now."

She picks it up and studies it. Her fingers moving over the paper. "I don't have to open it. I feel keys. You put keys in here."

That's all I put in the envelope. Two keys, both to my place. "You're not supposed to guess the gift before you open it."

She laughs at my mock frustration. "Are you asking me to move in with you?"

"I want you to give up your place and live with me, Lark. I want every today and tomorrow to be with you."

"I want that too." She rests both her hands on my shoulders. "I love you, Ryker."

I break then. This is all too good. Life can't be this good. I feel the emotion fighting to come out so I let it. A tear falls from my eyes. "I love you, baby. Let's go home so I can make love to my soon-to-be fiancée."

Epilogue

6 Months Later

Lark

"Holy fuck, Ryker," I scream. "You can't scare me like that. What the hell?"

He's nude. So am I. I just had a shower, a cool shower to beat the heat that's been hanging over the city for the past two weeks. I had left work before he did today. He's been putting in longer hours since the holiday campaign is set to launch next month. Ryker's back at Matiz and I couldn't be happier.

He's happy too knowing that Cremza is running smoothly under the guidance of the manager he hired.

"I'm sorry, Lark." He fiddles with something behind his back. I can see the reflection of something in the mirror behind him. "I know I promised I'd wait but shit, baby, please."

He drops to his knee then. My beautiful lover, the man I gave my heart to drops to his knee in the middle of our bathroom as I stand in front of him with my hair dripping all over my shoulders and down my body.

"Ryker," I whisper. "Are you going to do it now?"

He leans forward to wrap one of his arms around my waist to nudge me closer. "Come here, Lark. Come close to me."

I do. I step toward him, my toes touching his knee. "I love you, Ryker."

"I love you," he repeats before his lips graze my belly. "I love this little man, too. I love him so much."

I do too. I don't know him yet. Neither of us does, but we talk about him as if he's already here. Our son will be born in the fall. My doctor told us that he was most likely conceived around Valentine's Day. We didn't use a condom that night or any time since. I took my birth control pills, but the doctor said that they're not foolproof. We didn't care. We were overjoyed when we found out that we were going to have a baby. Our baby.

Ryker brings his other hand into view and opens it. I see the box. It's the box that he's kept hidden in the top drawer of the desk in his home office. I first saw it in May when I was looking for tape to wrap a gift for my mom for Mother's Day. I opened the small box without realizing what it was.

It's a beautiful diamond, a stunning solitaire in a white gold setting. I've never thought about what my ideal ring would look like until I saw the one Ryker picked just for me.

I didn't tell him I found it, but on Mother's Day, he asked me to marry him. I reminded him of our planned Christmas Day engagement and he kissed my still flat stomach and told me that sometimes we have to make compromises.

"I want you to be my wife now, Lark. I want us to be married when our baby comes."

I stare into his eyes. "I want to be your wife."

"I wake up every day more grateful than the one before. I get to love you. I get to raise a child with you. I get to grow old with you, Lark. Please marry me. Please let me be by your side forever."

I hold his hand while I lower myself to my knees. "If I say yes, when do you want to get married?"

"Next month." He kisses my hand. "I want you to marry me on my birthday."

"You want to share your birthday with our anniversary?" I look down at the still closed ring box.

"I finally felt like I was living when I met you, baby. What better way to celebrate my birthday than by marrying the woman I love? Will you marry me, Lark?"

I look into his eyes as I hear the box open. I feel the cool metal when he holds the ring against my fingertip. I nod. "Yes. I'll marry you."

"I can finally breathe now." He laughs as he slides the ring on.

"You knew I was going to say yes." I hold my hand up, admiring the ring. "This is beautiful, Ryker. I love it."

"You've seen it."

I shoot him a look. "What?"

"I've caught you twice snooping around my desk to look at the ring. You even tried it on once."

I did. I put it on my finger one morning when I thought he was still asleep. "I didn't mean to find it. It just happened."

"Do you hear that baby boy?" He presses his lips to my belly. "Your mom has no patience. When you get her a gift, you'll need to find a better hiding place than your dad's desk."

"Can we name him Benton, Ryker? Can our baby be Benton Moore?" I tilt my chin up, my eyes glued to his.

I see the smile in his eyes before it takes over his mouth. "You like it? I wasn't sure you were on board when I suggested it, but it's perfect. I want that for him, Lark. I want him to carry the name of his mother and his father, of both of us."

"I want your name too," I say quietly. "I want to be Lark Moore."

His kiss says it all. I'll be his forever and he'll be mine and three months from now we'll become a family. The family that neither of us could have expected a year ago, but both of us treasure forever with our lives.

THANK YOU

Thank you for purchasing my book. I can't even begin to put to words what it means to me. If you enjoyed it, please remember to write a review for it. Let me know your thoughts! I want to keep my readers happy.

For more information on new series and standalones, please visit my website, www.deborahbladon.com. There are book trailers and other goodies to check out.

If you want to chat with me personally, please LIKE my page on Facebook. I love connecting with all of my readers because without you, none of this would be possible. www.facebook.com/authordeborahbladon

Thank you, for everything.

Preview of TENSE

A Two Part Novel Series Featuring Nicholas Wolf

"Do you like it? Some people have said it's too long. It's actually quite thick when you're holding it in your hands, isn't it?" The tone is low and throaty, emanating somewhere from my right.

Such is the conversation on subway trains in New York City. You'd think I'd be oblivious to it all by now. Most of those who have lived here for decades have an innate ability to silence the staccato sounds of voices, traffic, and the underlying hum that is constantly hanging in the air in Manhattan.

For those of us who are considered fresh transplants, the timbres of the city are still part of its irrefutable charm. I never thought I'd get accustomed to the constant buzz of the traffic when I closed my eyes to sleep each night but now it's the lull that helps me drift off. I've only been here two years but I know that I'd long for the frenzied energy of this place if I ever decided to move back home to Florida.

"I'd like your honest opinion." I feel the slight pressure of a strong shoulder rub against mine. "Chapter seven is my personal favorite. Have you gotten that far yet?"

I glance down at the thick book resting on my lap. I know, without a doubt now, that he's talking to me. I've already had two, one-sided, conversations today about the book. One was with a woman waiting in line at the dry cleaners. The other was just fifteen minutes ago with the man who runs the bodega by my office. In both cases, I just smiled, nodded and listened to them rattle on about the awe inspiring detective novel I'm lugging around Manhattan with me.

"I haven't," I say quietly without looking at him.

No eye contact will make it easier for me to ignore him if he persists. I'm not a rude person but I do know how to protect myself with a perimeter of ignorance. Men give up easily if you pretend they don't exist. Most men do, that is. This one doesn't seem to be taking the hint.

"Have far are you?" A large hand brushes against my skirt. "You at least got past the first chapter, right?"

Physical touching is a no-no. I scoot more to my left, trying to gain even a few more inches in distance from him. This train is bursting at capacity with commuters. Part of that is the time of day and the other is the route.

It's early evening and I'm headed for Times Square, one of the few places in the city I'd be happy never seeing again. It's too much for me. There are too many people, too much noise, the smells overwhelming and the energy frenetic.

"I'm not trying to accost you." He laughs. It's a sexy growl and a few women actually turn to see the source. Judging by the way they linger when they look at him, he's not hard on the eyes.

"I'm just trying to get to a book signing," I confess, hoping he'll leave me alone if I tell him, politely, that I'm not looking to hook up. "I need to get this signed for my boss. It's a gift from his wife."

"You're hoping to meet the author? Nicholas Wolf? I heard the line for the signing was around the block already. People have been waiting all afternoon to meet him."

"Shit." I finally turn to look at his face. "You're not serious, are you?"

He's as good looking as I imagined him to be based on his voice. Seriously hot. Like seriously, I will give this man my number if he asks me for it, hot.

Black hair, blue eyes, and just the right amount of stubble on his face are the appetizer. His perfect teeth, rugged jaw and his lips, oh those lips, are the main course. He's wearing a wool coat and jeans so who knows what dessert is, but it would be delicious. I know it would be so delicious.

"I'm serious," he says. "If you get in line now, the store is going to close before you'll get that book signed for your boss."

I roll my eyes. "I don't get the appeal. I have no idea why Gabriel likes it so much. He told me to read it so I read the first chapter and…" I point my thumb towards the floor.

"Thumbs down?" He cocks a dark winged brow. "You didn't like it?"

"It's too wordy. I was too bored to finish it."

He stares at the book before he speaks again. "I take it Gabriel is your boss? You're getting it signed for him?"

I nod sharply.

"Give it to me. I'd like to show you something."

It's not my book and since we're moving at breakneck speed inside a subway car, it's not as though he can grab it and run. I slide it from my lap to his.

"What's your name?" he asks as his hand dives into a leather bag sitting on the floor at his feet.

I watch his every movement. "Sophia. My name is Sophia. What's your name?"

He pulls a silver pen from out of the bag and before I can protest, he opens the cover of the book and starts writing.

Well, shit. I bet it's his number. I'm not going to stop him. I'll just buy another book for Mr. Foster and keep this one for me.

He closes the cover of the book, slides the pen back into his bag and turns to look at me.

"My name is Nicholas. Nicholas Wolf."

Coming Early 2017

Preview of WORTH

A Two-Part Novel Duet Featuring Julian Bishop

I notice him immediately. It's impossible not to. Julian Bishop is the man of the hour, after all. This celebration, complete with expensive champagne and stiff-backed wait staff, has drawn the crème de la crème of Manhattan's social elite. It's the place to be tonight, and with a lot of crafty manipulation and a fair bit of luck, I'm standing in the midst of it, wearing a killer little black dress and diamond earrings I borrowed from a broker who has sold more than her fair share of apartments with Park Avenue addresses.

"I got you another glass of champagne, Maya."

I turn toward my date for the evening, taking the tall crystal flute from his hand. I enjoy a small sip while I look at his hands. They're adequate, not too large, and not too small. Those hands, along with the brief kiss he gave me when he picked me up tonight promise a night of passion that would be forgettable at best. He's nothing to write home about or to write about at all, for that matter.

"Thanks, Charlie," I purr. "Where's your drink?"

He nudges the sexy-as-all-hell, black-rimmed glasses up his nose with his index finger. He has a nerd with a side of male model look. That's what made me stop at his desk two weeks ago to ask if I could borrow his stapler.

I don't staple. If I did, I'm sure I'd find one in my desk, hidden underneath the three dresses and two pairs of shoes I have tucked in the drawer. I never know when a change of wardrobe is called for. A girl has to be ready for anything when she's trying to claw her way up the hierarchy of the Manhattan real estate market.

"I had one. That's my limit." He squints as he looks at the bar. "Is she here yet? I heard someone say she's going to make an entrance."

I heard someone say she's a dirty, dirty slut.

That someone was me. I said it to myself. She's far from dirty or slutty. She's a lawyer, Harvard educated, with looks to rival her brains. Jealousy is a filthy accessory and I don't wear it well at all.

"I don't think she's arrived." I turn back to where Julian's standing. He looks identical to the way he did when I first laid eyes on him. That was a year ago. I was helping a friend and he was offering her a job. Our paths crossed, the energy flowed and then he left. I never saw the man again.

I would have settled for one tumble in the sheets of his bed. A brief encounter would have satisfied my craving but it wasn't meant to be. He continued on his happily-ever-path and I swam the dating waters of Manhattan occasionally snagging a Charlie in my net.

"I'm going to mingle," I say it like I mean it. "I'll meet you back here in thirty."

Charlie looks down at his watch. It's not impressive. That's not Charlie's style.

"Thirty minutes, Maya." He touches the lenses of his glasses with two of his fingers before he points them right at me. "I'm going to have my eye on you."

Good for you, Cowboy.

I take my champagne, my spirit of adventure and my too tight black heels and I walk across the room. I took my time getting dressed tonight just for that one split second that we all live for. It's that moment when the man you imagine running naked through a field of daisies with or fucking in a back alley, turns and looks at you.

I've been planning this for two months.

Plotting every word I'll say when his eyes meet mine. I'm counting on him remembering me because I've been told I'm not easy to forget.

"Maya Baker." The voice behind me is unmistakably his. Warm with a hint of control, deep with a promise of pleasure.

I start to pivot at the sound of it. It's a beacon, a pull that is too strong to resist.

"Don't turn around." A hand, steady and determined, rests on my hip. The fingertips assert enough pressure to control my movement. "I don't recall seeing your name on the guest list."

Something's caught Julian's cock's attention. I can feel it pressing against me in the middle of this crowded room while we wait for his business partner, rumored lover and person I'd most like to lock in a closet for eternity to arrive. "I was a last minute addition."

"A welcome addition," he adds. "Are you enjoying yourself?"

I feel the undercurrent of desire. It was there last year when we met. It's stronger now.

"I am now." I push my fingers into his on my hip.

His chest lifts and falls. "I'm needed on the stage. You won't run away before we have a chance to talk, will you?"

I turn my head to look up at him. Black hair, ocean blue eyes and a face that would make any woman lock her office door to imagine a moment alone with him.

I've done it. Many women in Manhattan have.

"You're as handsome as ever, Julian."

He rounds me, his hand still holding mine. "You're more enchanting than the day we met, Maya. I've followed your career. I have a position I think you'd be interested in."

Coming 2017

ABOUT THE

AUTHOR

Deborah Bladon has never read a romance hero she didn't like. Her love for romance novels began when she was old enough to board the bus, library card in hand to check out the newest Harlequin paperbacks. She's a Canadian by heart, and by passport, but you can often spot her in New York City sipping a latte and looking for inspiration for her next story. Manhattan is definitely her second home.

She cherishes her family and believes that each day is a gift for writing, for reading, and for loving.

Printed in Great Britain
by Amazon